THREE DAYS

Visit us at www.boldstrokesbooks.com

THREE DAYS

by

L.T. Marie

2011

THREE DAYS
© 2011 BY L.T. MARIE. ALL RIGHTS RESERVED.

ISBN 13: 978-1-60282-569-7

THIS TRADE PAPERBACK ORIGINAL IS PUBLISHED BY
BOLD STROKES BOOKS, INC.
P.O. BOX 249
VALLEY FALLS, NY 12185

FIRST EDITION: OCTOBER 2011

CREDITS
EDITORS: VICTORIA OLDHAM, LEN BAROT, SHELLEY THRASHER
PRODUCTION DESIGN: STACIA SEAMAN
COVER DESIGN BY SHERI (GRAPHICARTIST2020@HOTMAIL.COM)

Acknowledgments

Writing my first book is a dream come true but wouldn't have been possible without the help of some very important people.

First of all, to BSB for taking a chance on me and believing in this story. Rad, the experience of getting to work with you was priceless, and I can never thank you enough for your guidance and patience.

To my editor, Victoria Oldham. Thanks for making me laugh during the editing process. You made my first experience enjoyable and surprisingly painless.

To my friend Peggy for helping me with my grammar before I even decided to send the manuscript to BSB. Oh yeah, and for teaching me how to use Track Changes.

To cover artist Sheri. Your work is amazing. You truly make Bold Strokes Books stand out.

And finally to Tina. You are the other half of my heart. *Ti Amo.*

For Tina,
For taking your biggest gamble on me.

CHAPTER ONE

"Fuck, I hate the desert." Wincing, Dakota squinted into the intense midday sun as she hurried across the tarmac at the Vegas airport. She pulled on her dark shades and yanked the bill of her white Nike ball cap lower. Three days in hundred-degree weather—could anything be worse?

And she'd thought the two-hour plane trip from Seattle on her way to the only place on earth she called hell with her five-foot, ten-inch frame squeezed into a seat in the "cattle call" section of the Boeing 737 would be the low point of her day. No such luck. By the time her section was called to board, she'd ended up sitting in a center seat with her knees nearly touching her chin. The uncomfortable trip left her agitated, and the heat and bright light only intensified the effect, producing a pounding headache that started the moment she stepped off the plane. The flight attendant had informed everyone that at noon the temperature had reached ninety degrees. Considering it was only Thursday, she figured by Sunday she'd be comatose.

"God, I'm going to kill Riann." Dakota threw her overnight bag onto the ground and yanked her long black hair back into a ponytail, pulling it through the loop in the rear of her hat. Her tank top was already soaked, a sheen of moisture turning her coffee-colored skin a shade darker. If she didn't have an air-conditioned hotel room to look forward to within the hour, she would have turned right around and caught the next available flight out of town. Instead, she stood in the never-ending taxi line as she tried to bite back the nausea that threatened with every shallow breath.

What the hell is Riann thinking, holding a bachelorette party in Vegas during August?

An alarm sounded in her bag, reminding Dakota of the call she needed to make now that she had landed. She reached for her BlackBerry and punched in a familiar number. By the fourth ring, she glanced at her watch, wondering why, at almost noon, no one was answering the phone. The man standing next to Dakota in line must have picked up on her simmering annoyance because he took a step back just as a familiar cheery voice answered.

"Hello, Santini's. May I help you?"

"Damn right you can help me, Peter. I thought you'd never pick up the damn phone."

"Oh, it's *you.* Look, missy, I'm kind of busy here. Maybe you shouldn't call during the lunch rush."

Peter Montori had been Dakota's maitre d' and right-hand man ever since she built her restaurant nearly eight years ago. She was well aware that without Peter the business probably would have never achieved the high profile it had today, and thanks to his expertise she could leave her restaurant without any worries. But the price of that expertise was putting up with his smart-ass remarks and occasional quick temper.

"Well, maybe if my second-in-charge could move a little faster, the phone wouldn't have to ring so long." She stifled a laugh, picturing Peter turning red. Sometimes the only way to deal with his temper was to make him mad enough to laugh.

"Oh, you did not just say that. You know I could just leave here right now and put Eddie in charge."

Dakota called his bluff. "Yeah, that sounds great."

Peter would never put Eddie in charge because Eddie couldn't organize his way out of a paper bag. Eddie Martinez was an incredible chef but, unfortunately, that was where his talents ended. "Why don't you do that, and during your time off, maybe you could go get those hair implants you've been wanting."

Dakota knew she had hit a nerve when Peter gasped. She laughed, imagining him standing there with one arm on his hip, the phone cradled between his head and his shoulder, and the towel he usually kept draped over his arm snapping at her in the air even though she was fifteen hundred miles away.

"Oh, very funny, smart-ass. That's it. I *will* put him in charge. You'll see. You'll be begging me to come back, especially after he forgets to turn the stove off *again* and burns the place dow—" Dakota heard another gasp from Peter, the tone different, regretful. "Oh, Dakota…honey…I'm so sorry. I—"

Her phone vibrated with another call, giving her an excuse to end the conversation. "Hey, Peter, I have another call. I know you're busy. Just call me if you have any problems."

"Sweetie, really. You know I would never—"

"Peter, it's okay. I'll call you tomorrow. Now, enjoy me not being there, and I'll see you soon."

"Okay then. Get going and try to have fun. You have a party to attend. Ciao."

Dakota clicked over to the other caller and said hello a little rougher than she intended. The unexpected memories had caught her off guard, and a familiar ache in her heart joined the pain in her head. *Fuck, fuck, fuck!*

"Well, hello to you too. I see someone's in a shitty mood this morning," her best friend Riann said.

"Why would you say that?"

"Oh, yes, we are cranky, aren't we? Let's see. You're in the desert, it's over a hundred degrees already, and the plane trip probably gave you a splittin' headache. How close have I come so far?"

"Right on all counts." Dakota sighed. "And stop rolling your eyes. I can hear it over the phone. Besides, I've already passed the headache stage. It's officially a migraine now."

"Oh, honey, it's that bad? I'm sorry," Riann said in a quieter voice.

Dakota rolled her suitcase closer to the curb when the line moved slightly forward. Just hearing Riann's voice helped her get her bearings again. Riann might give her a hard time when she thought Dakota was fucking up, but Riann was always there for her—even when she did screw up. "Are you *sure* you wouldn't rather marry me than Frank? You already know all my bad habits, you know my moods better than anyone else, and you know I'll be loyal to you forever."

Riann laughed. "Oh, baby, you know I would if I liked pu—"

"Stop...stop. God, you're bad."

"That's what Frank says. So, how close are you to the hotel?"

"Haven't even left the airport yet." Dakota looked at the line and groaned. "I might not get a cab until tomorrow."

"What! You have to meet Terry in less than half an hour. She'll bust a vein if you don't get there."

Her and me both. Dakota squeezed her eyes shut, as if that would make Riann's voice less piercing. "Will you stop worrying? And stop yelling. I have it all under control."

"No, you don't. I know you don't want to be there, but you agreed to come. Terry's going to rip you a new one for being late if you don't get moving."

"I'm in the damn cab line, Riann. Give me a break." Dakota's frustration was mounting because Riann was right. Knowing Terry, she was probably entertaining thoughts of bodily injury as they spoke. Like this was her fault! She looked around for some other means of transportation but couldn't see any alternative. She did, however, see a very attractive woman sitting on one of the airport benches applying a pretty shade of red lipstick to her full, luscious lips. She grinned when the woman puckered those lips and winked at her.

"Dakota, you still there?"

"Huh? Yeah, yeah, I'm here." Dakota dropped her gaze to the woman's plunging neckline. "Before I go, *Your Majesty*, anything I should I tell Terry when I get there?" As soon as she finished speaking, she could swear she heard Riann smile against the phone.

"Actually, since you mentioned it..."

Dakota recognized that hesitation. She wouldn't like anything Riann was about to say. "What have you done now, Riann, and will Terry blame me for it?"

"Oh, nothing, really. Just...well..." Riann's words tumbled out, as if she thought by saying them quickly Dakota might not lose what was left of her temper. "Since Pauline can't come because they won't give her the time off from work, I've invited my cousin Shawn to take her place, especially since the weekend is already paid for and we have an extra bed in Missy's room. Shawn is flying in with me this afternoon."

"What! Your cousin Sean is a dude. No guys allowed at the party, Riann. I thought we all agreed on that."

"Not that cousin. My other cousin Shawn—Shawn Camello—from Chicago. Not Sean O'Malley. Why the hell would I want him at my bachelorette party?"

"Okay, Riann, you've lost me. Who is Shawn Camello?" Dakota had known Riann since they were five years old and had met everyone in Riann's life, but she didn't recall a Shawn Camello.

"Seeing how you need to meet Terry in fifteen minutes, the story of Shawn and me will have to wait," Riann said. "Go do your superwoman thing and find a way to get there."

Dakota suddenly got the whole picture. If she'd never heard of Shawn, Terry didn't know about Shawn's existence either, and Miss Organization herself would blow a gasket at any last-minute changes. With Terry and her rigid timetable, Dakota would have to schedule regular bathroom breaks throughout the day.

"Oh, so the picture is finally coming together," Dakota said. "When exactly did you invite this mystery *cousin* of yours to the party?"

"Last week."

"What! You had all this time to tell Terry, and instead, you want me to do it at the last minute? Are you *crazy*?" Dakota tried not to attract any more attention than her restless pacing already had, but keeping her voice down when her head was splitting and her last nerve was frayed was impossible.

"Dakota, just do this for me, pleeeeease. I'll be your best friend."

"You're already my best friend." Dakota groaned. Hell, she could never say no to Riann, especially when she begged. She took a deep breath. "Okay, but you owe me, Riann."

"No, I don't. This makes us even for Donna and that mess—"

"Okay, okay, you're right. We're even," she said. *No need to bring that up.*

"Good, I'm glad we agree. Now get going before Terry places a bounty on your head."

Dakota sighed. "Okay, see you later tonight, bye."

An interminable five minutes later, Dakota finally made it to the front of the line and jumped into the next available cab, instructing the driver to take her to the MGM. She threw her head back against the seat and closed her eyes, happy for a few minutes' peace. When the cab lurched to a halt in front of the hotel, she still hadn't figured out how to break the bad news to Terry. A woman entering the lobby in a short summer skirt showing off a terrific pair of legs provided an excellent distraction. After all, she was in Vegas—she had to enjoy the beautiful landscapes, didn't she? She paid the driver, collected her bags, and hustled inside. As soon as she burst through the revolving doors, a blast of cool air slammed into her, the change from outside so drastic her stomach lurched. That little upset was nothing to the sinking feeling she got when she spied Terry talking to the concierge. Terry's forehead was creased and she was waving one arm to punctuate whatever she was saying. *Oh shit, she's already pissed and she doesn't even know about Shawn yet.*

"Hey, babe, glad you could finally make it." Terry stood on her toes to plant a kiss on Dakota's cheek. She was a good six inches shorter than Dakota, with piercing green eyes, reddish-blond hair, and a high, lilting voice similar to Riann's—Dakota's exact opposite in every way. Terry was not only Riann's cousin, but also her maid of honor and chief organizer for both the bachelorette party and Riann's wedding reception. "How was the flight?"

"Hey, yourself, and let's just say it was crowded." Dakota noted the list in Terry's hand. Yep, she'd been right about the bathroom breaks, but all in all she'd gotten off easy. She had originally been offered the maid-of-honor job but politely refused after informing Riann that no way in hell would she ever wear a bridesmaid's dress, or any type of dress, for that matter. She was touched that Riann had offered and insisted Riann hold the reception at her restaurant to make up for bailing on the MOH thing. She'd even volunteered to help Terry with the details involving food, flowers, and catering. "Sorry I'm late."

"No, you're not," Terry said. "I saw you cruising every woman in range."

"Yeah, well, I'm human." Dakota grinned and tilted her chin toward the list that Terry held in a death grip. "Is anyone else here yet?"

"Nice try changing the subject and no, not yet, but they will be by tomorrow morning. Remember, we're a day early."

"Right, yeah. Have you...talked to Riann?"

"No, why?" Terry folded her arms across her chest.

"Well, she told me to tell you we have an addition to the group."

"Are you *kidding* me?" Terry yelled, drawing stares from people walking by. "Who? And why the hell didn't she tell me herself?"

This was exactly the reaction Dakota expected. Riann could forget about being even in the debt department. "Uh—"

"Damn it. She knows all the plans are finalized." Terry looked like a stroke was imminent. They were starting to draw a crowd of amused and curious onlookers. "And don't make any excuses for her. When I see her—"

"Jesus, Terry, take it easy. It's my fault. She told me a few days ago to tell you and I forgot. I'm sorry, okay? But we can't change it now. Besides, they'll be arriving together in a few hours. So let's just take care of what we have to take care of and move on."

"Easy for you to say. Just what am I supposed to do? We already have all the tickets, the rooms are full, dinner reservations are done, and—"

"Stop! I understand. But since Pauline can't make it, Shawn can take her place and stay in Missy's room. It's covered."

"Wait a minute. She invited Sean? That doesn't make any sense. He's a guy. We said no guys." Terry crumpled her well-prepared list and tossed it onto the floor. "I quit."

Dakota started to laugh.

"What the hell's so funny?"

"I said the same thing. It's not Sean *O'Malley*. It's her cousin Shawn—S-H-A-W-N—Camello from Chicago, and that's all I know."

"Wait a minute." Terry looked as confused as Dakota had felt earlier. "I don't remember Riann ever mentioning a cousin named Shawn."

"It has to be on her mother's side." Dakota pointed to the list as Terry picked it up. Events appeared to be listed by day and time in neat columns. "Shawn's coming in with Riann. What time is the plane due?"

"It says here four. So I'll change reservations for dinner

tonight from three to four people and we can discuss the plans for the rest of the weekend before everyone else shows up. That's where *she* comes in," Terry said, smiling at the brunette sitting behind the concierge desk.

"Veronica Velasco," the woman said, extending a well-manicured hand to Dakota as she stood. "But my friends call me Ronnie."

Dakota had been so busy dodging Terry's verbal bullets she hadn't actually focused on the beautiful woman with a hint of Mediterranean in her features. *Wow. Do I qualify as a friend? Let's find out.* "Nice to meet you, Ronnie." Dakota held on to the outstretched hand while she slowly smiled into Ronnie's eyes. "I'm Dakota."

Ronnie's dark chocolate eyes flickered over Dakota's face and settled on her lips. "It's nice to meet you too, Dakota. Interesting name. I'll be sure to remember it. Let me know if I can do anything else to make your stay with us more pleasurable."

Dakota nearly shivered when the word *pleasurable* rolled off the concierge's tongue, as if she were running that tongue down the center of Dakota's chest. Maybe this weekend wouldn't be a complete loss after all. Not to mention Ronnie worked in the hotel. Had she hit the jackpot already? Suddenly she couldn't care less about the list Terry was waving in front of her face or the mysterious Shawn person who was arriving that evening. She was finding it difficult to pull her eyes away from Ronnie's gaze.

"Well, from what I can see by this list of activities you've arranged for us, it looks like our weekend is quite full. But I'm sure I'll have questions that will need answers later."

"I'm sure we'll be fine, Ronnie," Terry said impatiently. "Won't we, Dakota?"

Dakota snapped back to attention, feeling Terry tug her in the direction of the elevators. "I'm sure everything will be perfect, but we'll call if we have any problems."

"I'll be here, and of course if you need *anything*, just dial seven on your phone," Ronnie called, giving Dakota one last long, lingering look before returning to the stack of papers on her desk.

Terry dragged Dakota into one of the eight elevators that would take them to their rooms and, as soon as the large golden doors closed, said, "Could you just for once put a lock on your zipper?"

"What's your problem?" Dakota checked to see if her fly was closed, grinning when Terry laughed.

"You! You haven't been here more than ten minutes and already you're ready to bed the concierge. I swear to God, I've never met anyone like you, Dakota."

Dakota laughed. Not like she could deny it. "Okay, I did flirt *a little*, and maybe if you hadn't dragged me away from the front desk I could have worked out something with Ronnie."

"Oh, bullshit! Ten bucks says that by the end of this weekend you and Ms. Sexy Eyes downstairs find your way into a compromising position."

"So let me get this straight." Dakota hefted her bags as the elevator slowed. "If I take your bet, I'm betting against myself getting laid?"

"Exactly. So are you planning to take the bet?"

"Oh, yeah, you're on." She shook Terry's hand to seal the deal. "Let's just hope I lose." *What's another ten bucks? Hell, I'm in Vegas.*

CHAPTER TWO

Where are they? Their plane should have landed forty-five minutes ago." Terry paced in front of the arrivals board. "She's late, she's always late."

Dakota gripped Terry's shoulder, making her jump. "Jesus, will you calm down? It's not Riann's fault the plane is late."

Terry jammed her hands on her hips. "That's just like you, you know that? Sticking up for her all the time. You've always done that, even when we were kids."

"You know what? I can't talk to you when you're this wound up. I'm going to get something to drink." Dakota pointed in the direction of a nearby newsstand. "If their plane arrives before I return, just wait for me over there."

"Yeah...right...whatever," Terry murmured, staring at the arrival gate as if that would magically make Riann appear.

Twenty minutes later, Riann finally walked through the doors from baggage claim followed closely by a tall, willowy blonde.

"Hey, babe, how ya doin'," Terry said to Riann as she pulled her into a hug.

Riann introduced Terry and Shawn before glancing around the airport. "So, did Dakota come with you or is she still sleeping off her headache?"

Terry rolled her eyes. "Oh, no, she's off getting coffee. She told me to wait right here if your plane landed before she got back. Knowing her, she's probably already picked up some hot young thing in line at the Starbucks counter. She's been unstoppable since she arrived."

"Yeah, that sounds about right." Riann gave Terry a knowing grin. "Come on. Let's go find her before she disappears with some floozy for the weekend."

"Like it would only be one," Terry said with a laugh.

Shawn listened curiously while Riann and Terry talked about the mysterious Dakota. On the flight, Riann had described her as a playgirl, complete with details of her various conquests. Shawn hadn't registered much more than that, trying not to fidget and wondering why the hell she'd agreed to attend her cousin's bachelorette party. She wasn't interested in some woman's bed partners and just went through the motions, making the right noises and nodding at the right times. She had recently moved to Seattle and hadn't even had time to unpack yet, let alone jump on a plane and head to Vegas for the next three days.

She still couldn't quite fathom how Riann had just appeared one day at the bar where she worked, announcing excitedly that she was Shawn's cousin. She'd wanted to share Riann's excitement but wondered how anyone in her estranged family knew she even existed, let alone had moved to Seattle. Once Riann calmed down, she'd explained that Shawn's grandmother Amelia, the only relative Shawn ever spoke to, had slipped the news to her daughter, Riann's mother.

The two months she'd been in Seattle had been a whirlwind of finding an apartment, acquiring a job, then managing to strike up a relationship with Riann, whom she hadn't seen in over twenty years. Riann was clearly a true O'Malley. Shawn recognized the infamous traits immediately and thought about her mother, who had died from breast cancer when Shawn was young. Riann's quick wit, reddish-blond hair, and sharp tongue when provoked reminded her of all she had lost. The memories hurt. Would things have been different if Shawn had been more like her mother, more like Riann, instead of shy and reserved?

Shawn faded out of Riann and Terry's conversation when she noticed a very sexy Native American woman in form-fitting black jeans, a white sleeveless T-shirt, and dull black boots heading toward them. She almost didn't believe it when the tall, dark-haired woman veered in their direction. When the woman stared inquisitively at her, time stopped. Impossible, but she felt it all the same.

She couldn't look away as the attractive stranger slowly approached with cup in hand. She wasn't really walking but gliding across the floor. Shawn saw the scene in slow motion, as if watching an old-time movie at half speed. Everyone else in the room disappeared. The woman's dark brown skin and even darker eyes indicated her Indian heritage. The matching turquoise jewelry on her wrists and neck highlighted her lustrous skin. Shawn knew she should move, or at least breathe, but she was momentarily paralyzed. Every nerve in her body was on overdrive, and then to her astonishment, the woman stopped and leaned forward to hug Riann. Riann threw her arms around the taller woman and squealed.

Shawn blinked and realized Riann had been talking to her. "What?"

"Are you okay?" Riann asked.

"Yeah…I'm sorry, Riann. What did you say?"

"This is my best friend, Dakota." Riann tugged the good-looking stranger forward. "Dakota Riley, my cousin, Shawn Camello."

This is Dakota Riley? Oh, dear God! Shawn held out her hand but Dakota remained motionless, her coffee cup poised halfway to her lips. After waiting a few uncomfortable seconds, Shawn withdrew her hand. Dakota hadn't even blinked. Shawn was just about to retrieve her bag when Dakota suddenly grabbed the bag, brushing her hand over Shawn's in the process.

"Here, let me get that," Dakota said quietly. "Nice to meet you, by the way."

"Yeah, same here," Shawn muttered. Tall, dark hair, deep voice. Could Dakota be any sexier? Three days with this woman would be either heaven or, if she didn't get hold of her hormones soon, hell.

As Terry led the way to the exit, Shawn walked silently beside Dakota. When they passed the Starbucks counter, a short redhead waved and winked mischievously at Dakota. Riann smirked while Terry burst out laughing. Dakota did little more than nod, which was surprising. After all Riann's stories, she'd expected the infamous "love 'em and leave 'em" Dakota Riley to be more arrogant, more of an operator. Instead, she seemed almost embarrassed by the barista's attention and her friends' reactions. When Dakota just kept walking, Shawn was aware of taking her first deep breath since she'd stepped off the plane.

❖

Dakota stood nervously by the curb waiting for a cab with the group and drove her hands deep into the pockets of her jeans to hide her fidgeting. Directly in front of her Shawn provided an interesting view of her firm ass outlined perfectly in a pair of skimpy beige shorts. By the time one of the attendants finally whistled them over, Dakota was sweating profusely, but it had nothing to do with the temperature.

She was out of sorts, caught off guard by the new addition to the party. Besides being drop-dead gorgeous, Shawn had a way of appraising Dakota that not only made her uncomfortable but nearly brought her to her knees. Every time Shawn looked in her direction, she wanted to flee. Shawn didn't just look at her—she made her feel like she was a specimen squirming under a microscope and Shawn's x-ray eyes could see right through her. Most women regarded her as a prospective date or maybe a one-night stand because that's the image she projected. Not Shawn.

When those laser blue eyes shot her way, she felt almost naked. She didn't like the sensation.

Now she was driving herself crazy trying to figure out how she was going to deal with her unusual response to Shawn for the next three days. On top of all that, she needed to consider her reaction, or lack thereof, to the barista at the Starbucks counter. When did a woman *ever* flirt with her and she not flirt back? She was in Vegas, for Christ sakes! Women were everywhere, thousands of them. She was supposed to flirt. To meet one here or there and take her back to her room if the situation presented itself. It was who she was. Who she always planned on being. What the fuck was wrong with her?

"Dakota?"

"Yeah...what?" Dakota dragged her gaze away from Shawn. Riann stood in front of her with her hands on her hips, looking annoyed.

"There are two groups before us. We've got to wait ten minutes for a van," Riann said.

Dakota looked at all the luggage at Riann's feet. "Maybe if you'd packed for a weekend instead of a month, we wouldn't have to wait for something the size of a Mack truck to take us all to the hotel."

"Ha, ha. I see you're already trying to charm Shawn with your comedic abilities. Don't fall for it, Shawn," Riann said playfully.

While they debated, a cabbie jumped in and loaded Riann's luggage into his trunk and placed the rest on the front seat.

"Tell you what," Dakota said, "it's too hot for all of us to cram into one cab. Why don't you and Terry take this one, and I'll ride back with Shawn." To forestall any more discussion, she grabbed Shawn's suitcase and headed for the next cab in line.

A pretty blonde placed a small hand on Dakota's arm and smiled up at her. "Excuse me. Would you like to share a cab? I overheard you saying you were going to the MGM."

"Thanks," Dakota said with her most charming smile,

ignoring Riann's eye roll. "I appreciate the offer, but my friends need my services. Maybe I can make it up to you with a drink later?"

The blonde nodded knowingly, said, "I'll hold you to that," and headed for the next cab in line.

Terry and Riann piled into the one in front while Dakota held open the rear door of the second one for Shawn. "Ready?"

Shawn slid into the back and Dakota followed.

"You didn't need to escort me," Shawn said.

"It's no problem. Riann and Terry can use the time to hash out some last-minute details while we become acquainted."

"Really? You're pretty noble."

Shawn hadn't said much since their plane landed, but Dakota knew sarcasm when she heard it. "What do you mean?"

"That blonde back there had more than just a ride in mind. I'm surprised you declined."

"Why are you surprised?" Dakota straightened.

Shawn shrugged. "I just would have thought someone like you—"

"Someone like me? What do you know about me?"

Dakota looked taken aback, which wasn't the reaction Shawn had expected from the carefree playgirl Riann had described so vividly on the plane. Why had she said anything? She didn't care if Dakota flirted with every woman in Vegas. Did she? And she wasn't usually bitchy. Being around Dakota stirred up feelings she didn't like. "Never mind. Forget it. It's none of my business. Sorry."

Dakota stared blankly out the cab window. "I guess you're right."

"Excuse me?"

"About the woman," Dakota said. "Ordinarily I would have accepted her offer."

"Why did you decline?" Shawn asked, more than curious. She was really interested.

"Because I wanted to get to know you better."

Dakota sounded sincere. Had Shawn misjudged her? Maybe Riann had exaggerated. She ought to know appearances didn't always tell the truth. "Are you regretting your choice?"

"No. Of course not." Dakota shot her a smile, the cocky look back again. "I got to ride alone with you, didn't I?"

There was the playgirl Riann had described. And she'd almost let herself get pulled in with the old "I want to get to know you" line. God, when would she ever learn?

The cab abruptly halted in front of the MGM. "Dakota, you don't have to explain yourself to me. You are who you are. Thanks for the company."

Shawn climbed out of the cab and didn't look back.

Chapter Three

H ow was the ride?" Riann asked as she held the lobby door
open.

"Informative," Shawn said, and left it at that. She didn't
want to talk about Dakota. She just wanted to get up to the room.
Out of the corner of her eye, she caught Dakota checking her out.
Didn't she ever stop? The look wasn't much of a compliment,
considering that Dakota noticed most women. Like a mind reader,
Terry asked Riann the question that had plagued Shawn since her
arrival.

"Hey, Riann, have you thought about the sleeping
arrangements for tonight? We have two double beds in our room
and Dakota has a king. Where's Shawn supposed to sleep?"

Shawn tensed. No way would she bunk with Dakota. The
woman was way too attractive. She couldn't imagine spending
time alone with Dakota in a hotel room when her body wasn't
listening to her head. No. No way. She'd sleep in the lobby first.

"Shawn can have my bed," Riann said. "I'll share Dakota's
bed."

Shawn sighed in relief but Dakota, who had just joined them,
looked peeved.

"And what if I don't want to share a bed with you?" Dakota
asked.

"You have no choice tonight, Dakota. So suck it up. You'll

just have to wait one more night before cashing in on that notorious Riley charm."

Shawn laughed along with Terry, although Riann and Terry did seem to be having a little too much fun at Dakota's expense. After all, the woman was single, and so what if she was a player? Maybe Riann and Terry were a little jealous. Hell, maybe she was too. She hadn't had many dates lately, although that was pretty much her choice. Maybe she should start thinking about female company now that she'd moved to a new place. Just the thought of dating, though, made her stomach burn. Being around Dakota wasn't such a good idea—not if she wanted to keep her hard-won self-esteem intact. She took the key Riann extended to her, grateful to be able to escape.

"Thanks, I'll go get settled in." Shawn picked up her luggage.

"You need some help?" Dakota asked.

"No, thanks." Shawn turned abruptly and headed for the elevators, feeling Dakota's gaze follow her. She was probably being unreasonable. Dakota was only being polite, but chivalry usually came with an agenda attached. She'd had enough of that in the past, when she'd always been just a pretty face to women who liked to be in charge. She didn't need any reminders of her failed relationships, and Dakota's macho attitude was seriously getting on her nerves. If the woman didn't stop opening doors for her or volunteering to pick up her luggage, she might go postal. Three more days of this? What a disaster.

❖

Dakota looked at her watch for the tenth time during dinner. Across from her, Terry and Riann talked nonstop about the weekend plans. Shawn sat next to her, hardly speaking and pushing her salad around on her plate.

Dakota pretended to be engrossed in the conversation but instead focused on Shawn's leg against hers in the tight booth.

She caught a hint of the unique smell that she had already come to associate with Shawn, the scent of spring flowers on a rainy day. When Shawn began laughing at one of Terry's party stories and unconsciously brushed a hand over Dakota's, Dakota was tongue-tied. Her unusual social ineptness left her uncomfortable and struggling to find her game. Normally another woman's touch would have given her the perfect opportunity to strike up a conversation. Shawn's deep, throaty laugh was inviting, like a fire on a cold winter's night. She needed an icebreaker, but every thought in her head suddenly sounded like a line. Maybe because that was who she portrayed herself to be—someone who resorted to a few party lines and had no way of having a meaningful conversation without sex being the ultimate goal. What about Shawn made her keep questioning her actions, anyhow? Her approach with women had always worked before.

She glanced at Shawn again, this time noticing how she gently placed a few strands of hair behind her ear. The act itself wasn't necessarily the most erotic thing she had ever witnessed, but a slow beat pulsed between her legs. She gulped and quickly adjusted herself in her seat to alleviate the pressure. Guess that answered that question. Shawn turned her on and she wasn't even trying. Damn, that was dangerous.

"You know, Terry, you shouldn't be worrying so much about all the details," Dakota said abruptly. Between Terry complaining for the fifth time about keeping everyone on schedule and her totally foreign reaction to Shawn, she couldn't take any more. "Ronnie knows what she's doing and has everything under control. Why don't you relax and enjoy dinner before the craziness starts?"

"Oh? And how do you know everything will be *fine*?" Terry shot back. "Just because you want to sleep with the concierge doesn't mean she knows what she's doing."

"Huh?" Riann stared at Terry, then Dakota. "Who the hell is this concierge, and why don't I know about her?"

"She's nobody, Riann. Not the way Terry means." Dakota

could practically feel Shawn freezing up beside her, and for no good reason. She hadn't even been thinking about Ronnie as possible company, and ordinarily she would have been. Ever since the cab ride with Shawn, she'd been replaying her parting words. *You are who you are.* She knew the image she wanted to project. Carefree, casual, no strings. At least that's what she'd always thought, until Shawn had her questioning what she really wanted people to think. Her head hurt just imagining what Shawn must think of *this* conversation. Hoping to lighten the mood, she said, "Terry's just sexually frustrated, so she's taking it out on me."

"I am *not* frustrated," Terry snapped. "I'll have you know I have just as much sex as you. I'm just more discreet about it."

Laughing, Dakota called her bluff. "Oh, really? You're discreet. Let's see. What about Jerry, Pat, oh yeah, and Philip. Let's not forget Philip, because he was one of my favorites."

Dakota ducked as a cloth napkin flew across the table at her face. She grabbed a sugar packet and tossed it at Terry, who deflected it, almost hitting Shawn in the process.

"Sorry about that, Shawn." Dakota flushed, embarrassed that she had allowed Terry's comment to rile her. What the fuck was wrong with her? She usually took Terry's comments about her sex life as a compliment.

"Okay, children," Riann said, holding up her hands to signal a stop. "Knock it off before you embarrass Shawn any more and get us all thrown out of here."

"Sorry," Dakota muttered.

"She started it," Terry added, and everyone laughed.

"Well, are you going to tell me who this woman is?" Riann asked again.

Dakota shrugged sheepishly. "I told you. Just someone I talked to for a few minutes. No one important."

"Whatever! I guess the blonde at the airport was nobody either," Terry said, bumping Dakota playfully with her foot.

"Blonde?" Riann said. "Oh, yeah, I forgot about her." Riann

pointed her fork at Dakota. "So what about the concierge, and don't play games with me. You know I'll find out, and you know I won't let up until I do. Why all the secrecy?"

Dakota glanced at Shawn, who was staring at her along with Terry and Riann. She couldn't read what was behind Shawn's blank expression, which unsettled her. Usually she read women easily. She could tell by the way they walked, the way they talked, the way they leaned their head just the right way if they were interested. But Shawn had been like a closed book, entirely unreadable, from the moment they met at the airport. The more she found Shawn a mystery, the more she wanted to know about her.

"The blonde was just looking for conversation, and Ronnie was helping Terry with the arrangements. I was just being friendly." She signaled for the waiter for another beer, hoping to change the direction of the conversation. She wasn't a kiss-and-tell kind of person, even though she didn't keep her dates and dalliances from her friends. With Shawn sitting right next to her, though, she didn't want to talk about the likelihood of hooking up with Ronnie or anyone else. She could practically feel Shawn branding her as a shallow player.

"Uh-huh—friendly." Terry grinned. "Maybe you should tell Riann and Shawn about our little wager, Dakota. They might want to get in on the action."

"What wager?" Riann asked.

Dakota wanted to strangle Terry with her napkin. She normally enjoyed the childish banter with Terry, but right now she wanted her to drop the subject. Why couldn't she just let it go? Dakota listened uneasily while Terry explained the bet and Riann added money to the wager. Shawn cleared her throat and shifted a bit farther away from Dakota on the bench. She didn't participate in the bet but did change the topic by asking Riann how she was feeling about her big day.

Finally off the hook, Dakota drifted while the others discussed the details of the upcoming nuptials for the millionth time. Shawn had a nice voice—sensuous and full, kind of like her body. Dakota's mind wandered a little farther down that path. What would it be like to have that soothing voice coax her to orgasm?

Riann kicked her under the table. "Dakota, are you okay?"

"Yeah, fine. Why?"

"I don't know. You just seem...pouty."

"I'm not being *pouty*. I'm just tired and I haven't gotten rid of that heat headache yet."

Shawn half turned, the tension easing from her body. The little bit of worry in her eyes made Dakota feel better.

Riann flashed a wicked grin. "If you still aren't feeling well, why didn't you say something? Why don't you go get some sleep? I'm sure the rest of us will find *something* to do."

"I'm fine," Dakota said. All of a sudden, she didn't want to be left out of the activities and lose the chance to spend more time with Shawn. "Okay, you two, spill. What's going on in those crazy heads of yours?"

Riann glanced over at Terry, then back to Dakota as they said in harmony, "Strip club."

Dakota laughed. "Already?"

"Yep. We're going to check out a few of the clubs tonight. Shawn, you're invited, of course." Riann straightened up with a mock-serious expression. "I just want to do some reconnaissance to see which one would be fun for the whole group to hit Saturday night, so tonight is *purely* academic."

"Oh, please. Half-naked men dancing two feet away at eye level?" Dakota snorted, thinking she should be happy to be left out after all. She could escape and find some entertainment more to her liking. Maybe she could hook up with Ronnie, even if she did lose the bet everyone had been so happily discussing. "*Purely* academic, my ass! You want to check out the guys wearing Speedos and bow ties."

Riann and Terry sighed languidly. Shawn laughed.

"Yeah," Riann said. "So we understand if you don't want to go, honey. How about you, Shawn?"

Dakota perked up. *Yeah, Shawn, how about you?*

"Sounds like fun. I'm in." Shawn gave Terry a small smile, but something about the way she ducked her head and focused on her salad said she wasn't all that comfortable with the idea. And just like that, Dakota ditched her plans to escape and find company for the night.

"I'm in too. I don't have anything against hot, sweaty bodies." Dakota thought she caught a flicker of a smile from Shawn. Funny, that little bit of connection made her feel better than just about anything had all day.

CHAPTER FOUR

The cab pulled up in front of another strip club—the fifth one in two hours. Shawn glanced at her watch, the hands reading after one, early Friday morning. She wasn't looking forward to another loud, smoky bar. And by the displeasure on Dakota's face, neither was she.

"Oh, God, not another one." Dakota groaned.

Terry giggled with excitement.

"Come on, Dakota." Riann patted Dakota's thigh. "I promise this will be our last one tonight."

Shawn wasn't sure she believed that. Riann and Terry seemed to be having a great time and, after all, wasn't that what this three-day bachelorette extravaganza was all about? Riann having the time of her life before she settled down? The night hadn't really been all that bad because Dakota seemed to be paying close attention to her wherever they went. Every scan with those dark eyes was as intimate as a touch. She kept waiting for Dakota to start a conversation, but she never did.

Shawn caught sight of several scantily clad female dancers chatting up the patrons outside the club. One particular brunette dressed in black leather shorts with matching top and boots, complete with whip, really appealed to her. Without the costume she looked a little like Dakota. Shawn laughed inwardly. Busted. It was easy to get caught up in the sights and sounds of this hot, erotic town at midnight, and the attractive company didn't hurt. Damn—as the brunette seductress leaned forward and kissed another female dancer, her tongue darting into the other woman's mouth as their bodies pressed together, Shawn instantly became wet. They were hot all right. If she could have spared twenty dollars, she wouldn't have minded a dance from that particular one. She squirmed uncomfortably in her seat.

"What do you think, Shawn? One more?" Riann asked as she climbed out of the cab.

"Sure. This one looks more interesting than the last two. Don't you think so, Dakota?"

Dakota's head whipped in Shawn's direction and she grinned. "Yes, much more interesting."

Dakota seemed to comprehend her meaning instantly, but Terry and Riann were oblivious. They obviously knew Dakota went for women, and Shawn assumed Riann knew she did too. Oh, well. It really didn't matter since she didn't plan to pick anyone up tonight.

She waited for everyone else to climb out of the cab while Dakota held the door, continuing to give her that conspiratorial smile. Shawn had a hard time not smiling back. She loved being the focus of a woman's attentions, maybe because as she grew up, no one really *had* noticed her for more than her looks. Dakota was attentive and drop-dead sexy, which was exactly what had gotten her into trouble in the past. Women were always gallant with her, until they got what they wanted—usually sex. That wouldn't happen this time. Dakota was very easy on the eyes, but casual company would be all she got, tonight or any night.

Shawn didn't even look behind her as they walked into the club. She didn't need to. She could still smell the familiar musky aroma. Dakota was near. Not even the smell of sex that mingled with the alcohol inside the crowded club could drown the unique scent she already associated with Dakota.

The atmosphere inside the bar was hotter, stickier, than the hot Vegas night, the heat so intense that bodies appeared to melt into one another. For a few seconds, the flashing strobe lights blinded her and the loud music reverberating off the wooden walls of the barn-style room disoriented her. This wasn't like the other clubs they had visited over the past few hours. No male dancers were within eyeshot, just beautiful women of all shapes and sizes gliding up and down poles, dancing erotically onstage or giving a few of the patrons lap dances in the back corner.

While the group headed for the bar, Shawn caught Dakota's expression out of the corner of her eye, and the sudden transformation stunned her.

Dakota stalked the crowd, her gaze darting back and forth between the dancers, her body taut and tense. Her eyes were intense, dark and sharp. She trembled slightly, as if trying to cage some powerful urge. Shawn recognized the signs of a hunter stalking its prey.

Dakota's hot gaze swung back to her, and the heat blasted her before Dakota stared back at the gyrating dancers. Shawn took a deep breath to quell the butterflies in her stomach and the scorching arousal that ambushed her. She turned away to catch her breath and waved to get the bartender's attention. Mostly she just needed to escape for a few seconds. She didn't want to see what happened when Dakota's reins snapped and she captured her quarry.

❖

Dakota inhaled deeply, the smells of alcohol and sex oozing from every corner of the room. This was more like it. Weddings and people's feelings weren't her thing—this was her element. Sex, pure and simple, wrapped in an array of incredibly hot packages. Comfortable and confident, she surveyed the room for possible entertainment. She eyed a particular dancer, a sensual cowgirl slinking up and down one of the poles along the far wall, and imagined herself in place of the prop. The woman slid seductively around the pole, running her center firmly along the gleaming metal. Dakota's stomach clenched. Yeah, she really wouldn't mind being that pole. But the scene in her mind flicked forward and the woman clinging to her was Shawn. She was naked and Shawn was gliding her warm, wet center over her thigh. Whoa!

Dakota propelled herself back into reality, quickly surveying the room to find Shawn and the others conversing at the bar. The all-too-real daydream had her insides tied in knots and left a lingering surge between her legs. But when Shawn glanced up to meet her eyes, surprisingly the erotic thoughts faded, leaving her with a sudden sense of guilt. She had no reason to feel guilty—after all, it was just a daydream, albeit a very pleasant, erotic one. So why was her mind in a state of rebellion? Riann raised her glass in salute and Dakota knew the answer. Shawn was Riann's cousin, and Dakota's well-known habit of leaving broken hearts in her wake wouldn't sit well if Shawn happened to be one of the victims. How could she entertain thoughts of sleeping with Shawn when Riann was the closest thing to a family she had? She couldn't risk losing anyone else. Protecting the few personal connections she allowed herself was one reason she never spoke about what had truly transpired the night her world tumbled down around her.

Besides, she liked to keep her public and private lives separate. Her equation was simple. No emotion—no strings—no complications. And no messing with friends, family, or friends of same. That put Shawn off-limits.

She had to keep her distance. And although the image of Shawn moaning beneath her nearly made her buckle, consequences be damned, she refused to ignore her own rules, even for someone as hot as Shawn.

"Thanks," Dakota said absently, taking the beer Riann held out.

"You okay?" Riann asked.

"Yeah. Fine."

"You looked a little spooked."

"Nope. Couldn't be better." Dakota carefully avoided looking at Shawn.

"If you say so." Riann pointed to a sign near a back staircase. *No Men Allowed.* "Looks like that's where the action is."

They moved through the mass of bodies as a group, and a large African American bouncer with a name tag reading *Jackson* pinned across the left breast pocket of his black T-shirt unhooked a black velvet rope blocking the foot of the stairs and waved them up. The second floor rocked with loud, pumping music and the heat from hundreds of screaming women who surrounded the twenty- by twenty-foot stage. Some were placing money in the male dancers' Speedos while others got private lap dances near the rear of the stage.

Smoke emitting from two dry-ice machines located on the stage made it difficult to see. Dakota could have sworn Shawn placed a hand lightly on her back while following her through the tightly packed room.

Once they reached a free booth, Dakota took orders for more drinks and shouldered her way up to the bustling bar, ordering two Coronas, one Long Island iced tea, and a club soda for Shawn. Shawn hadn't had a drink all evening. Was that a usual choice or did she just not feel like letting loose in front of people she didn't know very well? Shawn wasn't easy to figure, which made her all the more interesting. Dakota retrieved the drinks just in time to make it back to the booth to find a bunch of male dancers had gathered around Riann and a very eager Terry.

A muscular blond fireman took twenty bucks from Terry to give Riann a lap dance, while Terry found a darker-haired version for her own pleasure. Shawn sat quietly off to the side, watching them with the same amused look on her face she had sported much of the evening.

"Here you go." Dakota handed Shawn her drink, which she accepted with a smile. Dakota really liked the way Shawn smiled. She leaned against the booth right next to her, admiring her cleavage.

"Thanks."

"Any time. Are you enjoying yourself?"

"It's okay. Are you?"

"Yes, but I just care that Riann is enjoying herself. It is her weekend, after all."

"That's sweet of you, Dakota."

Dakota paused, searching for the right words. She was glad for the darkly lit room because she felt herself blush. This was their first real conversation. She didn't want to blow it. "Lap dances not your thing?"

Shawn looked up, locking eyes with Dakota. "Not really. I'm more of a one-on-one type of person."

"Really?" Dakota dropped her voice an octave, although she was still nearly shouting over the pounding music and screaming women. "That's good to know. Maybe—" A burly male dancer in a police uniform and clutching handcuffs pushed his way between her and Shawn. He leaned down and whispered something into Shawn's ear that made her look uneasy. Dakota scowled at the guy.

The dancer didn't get the message, pumping his hips in Shawn's direction and giving her a *Hey, baby* look. Shawn didn't seem offended, though she didn't look particularly interested. As the dancer climbed into Shawn's lap, Dakota thought she'd give anything to trade places with him. Then she reversed the roles in her head and imagined Shawn once again as the dancer, thrusting her hips in Dakota's direction, her erect nipples only inches from Dakota's awaiting mouth. She nearly groaned out loud as heat pounded through her, settling firmly between her legs.

Shawn smiled faintly at the dancer and clearly mouthed the words "No, thank you." Either the guy didn't hear her over the loud music or didn't care, because he kept gyrating astride Shawn's lap. Shawn braced her hand on the large man's chest, stopping him from pinning her to the seat. "No, thank you," Shawn yelled, louder this time.

Dakota refused to sit there and watch him crawl all over

her, especially if she didn't want him to. She'd rather have her fingernails pulled out one at a time—slowly.

"The lady said no. Take the hint and get lost." Dakota gripped the dancer's shoulder to remove him from Shawn's lap.

He was obviously clueless because as soon as she touched him, he rose and threw one of his muscular arms around her. "Well, how about you, then, sweetie? In for a little action?"

She glanced at his arm, wondering if the guy realized just how close he was to having her rip his arm off and beat him with it. *It's either that or the fake baton strapped to his hip.*

"Um, Dakota," Shawn said, clearly stifling a laugh, "you might not want to take him on."

Dakota tried hard not to punch the guy, even though he outweighed her by fifty pounds. "What," Dakota said in a low voice, "I should let him paw you?"

Shawn's lips parted as if she were surprised, and she gave Dakota a downright smoldering look. "Hey, I appreciate you worrying about me, but I don't think he's dangerous. Except maybe to you."

Dakota pulled away from him, and when he followed with his arms open wide, she planted her right hand firmly in the middle of his chest. "No, thanks, buddy. I'm not in the mood tonight or any night."

"Something wrong?" He pumped his hips even faster.

"Look, we're not interested. Go away."

"Oh, come on, honey. Women only come here for two reasons," he said sweetly, running a hand down Dakota's arm.

Dakota clenched her fists, counting to ten. "Well, I'm here for reason number three. Now, for the last time, get lost."

Finally the dancer scowled and gave up. When he was out of sight, she slid into the space next to Shawn. "You okay?"

"Yeah, thanks."

"No problem. I'm glad I could be of service."

Dakota sensed a moment of truce and decided it was time to test the old Riley charm. Better to know what her chances were than keep driving herself crazy wondering if Shawn was up for an infamous Vegas hook-up. "Since this doesn't seem to be your thing either, would you like to get out of here and go someplace private where it's quieter? I know this great place—"

Shawn held up a hand. "No, thank you."

"Hey, I just thought—"

"You thought…what? That if you rescued me from a harmless dancer I would throw myself into your arms? I appreciate the gesture, but I don't need protecting. I've been on my own a long time and I'm quite capable of taking care of myself. But thanks for the drink all the same." Shawn picked up her jacket and stood. "Excuse me—bathroom."

Dakota stared after Shawn's retreating figure. "Fine, I'm outta here."

She found Riann getting a lap dance from a wiry dancer in a construction outfit. "I've had enough fun for one night," she whispered in Riann's ear. "See you in the morning."

She jogged down the wooden steps, trying to push her way through the bustling downstairs bar, which was proving difficult. Her body still hadn't quieted down after imagining Shawn in her lap, and the heavy beat inside the room escalated the insistent pounding between her thighs. Her push-pull attraction to Shawn notched up her frustration another level, so both her body and her head were ready to explode.

The whole thing with Shawn totally confused her. She'd never needed to chase a woman. She wasn't even attracted to women who didn't let her know loud and clear they were available. If they made the first move, she didn't have to be responsible for anything that happened. Plenty of women were always interested, but not Shawn. She was aggravating, standoffish, and clearly uninterested. And she was driving her out of her mind. Must be the heat. She couldn't think of another reason she'd let someone who didn't want to play get under her skin.

The room was so full Dakota was practically at a standstill. When she attempted to edge around a big guy wearing army fatigues, he yelled something about a lasso and suddenly a thick leather rope pinned her arms to her side. "Hey! What the fuck?" She gripped the rope with both hands and was about to yank it when she saw who was holding the other end.

The cowgirl who had been gliding up and down on the pole earlier inched down the rope, one hand after another, a predatory look in her blue eyes. Her expression was distinctly different from the almost bored one she'd possessed while dancing onstage less than an hour ago and was a lot like the smoldering look Shawn had thrown her upstairs.

Shawn. Dakota gulped, imagining Shawn slithering toward her. She wanted it to be Shawn. Her skin tingled at the image of Shawn in the cowgirl's place. But Shawn wanted nothing to do with her. She'd made that abundantly clear. The memory of Shawn dismissing her was all the encouragement she needed to concentrate on the dancer just inches away. Dakota licked her lips.

"Name?" The dancer stroked Dakota's arm.

"Dakota." Her words came out a choked whisper.

"It suits you. You look hot, Dakota. Interested in a dance?"

Damn right she was hot. She'd been on fire all evening. Shawn did that to her. Shawn had a way of fanning the fuel of her desire with as little as a smile. *Damn it. Forget Shawn for a second and focus!*

Dakota nodded as she focused on the sexy blonde's ass and trailed willingly behind her toward the center of the room like a roped calf. Mesmerized, she forgot the hundreds of eyes staring at them as the dancer positioned her in a large padded chair with a high wooden back.

The dancer slowly climbed into Dakota's lap and undulated to the music, her crotch inches from Dakota's face. She kept Dakota glued to her seat with her glistening body, rotating her hips to the blaring techno beat. Dakota couldn't take her eyes off the red star tassels that barely covered the dancer's nipples. She watched in fascination as they swayed in counterpoint to the blonde's hips. When one swinging tassel grazed her lips, she caught it between her teeth and gently tugged, careful not to pull it free. Her hands itched to caress the pale, smooth skin rubbing up and down against her chest, but touching without permission was the fastest way to be ejected from the club. The tease was all part of the game, and she was enjoying every agonizing second of it.

"Do you like what you see, Dakota?" the dancer asked, pushing farther into Dakota's lap.

"Yes, very much."

"Feel me. Give me your hands."

Dakota followed the gentle command without hesitation, clasping the dancer's waist. The dancer grasped Dakota's hands and slowly drew them up to just under her swaying breasts.

Dakota swallowed hard as the tense muscles rippled beneath her fingertips. She'd received lap dances before, but never from someone quite so skilled. This dancer was wreaking havoc on her, and each gentle skim of her hips and barely perceptible brush of her fingertips pushed her closer to eruption. Dakota's stomach tightened. She was so hard, the pressure against the seam of her jeans was becoming unbearable.

At that point she didn't care who watched. The hoots and hollers had faded the moment the dancer had roped her, but Dakota knew the crowd was still there, still watching. Just the thought of other people getting off on her getting off turned her on even more. When the woman's taut abdomen rubbed against the soft cotton of her shirt, Dakota groaned. Crap, she was primed and ready for take-off. Her nipples hardened instantly and the familiar stirring between her legs intensified. She was a minute away from a full-blown explosion. As if sensing her readiness, the blonde ran her hands over Dakota's chest, rubbing in small, firm circles over her nipples.

"Oh, God." Dakota groaned and arched into the torturous caress. She closed her eyes, absorbing the feel and smell of the woman grinding against her. She tried to fight the tingling sensation that slowly worked its way down into her pelvis but was losing the battle, quickly.

"How you feeling, baby?" the dancer whispered.

"Like I'm going up in flames." Dakota panted.

The dancer laughed.

The music changed to a slower beat and the lights dimmed. The onlookers faded into the background—all Dakota registered was the dancer writhing in her lap. With each pass of her hips, the blonde pressed farther into Dakota's crotch. She gripped the leather arms of the chair so hard she was sure she'd leave permanent marks.

A flash of Shawn's face popped up behind her eyelids, and her hips bucked into the woman astride her lap. She pictured Shawn in the dancer's place, grinding against her, and the first warning spasms ignited. The blonde picked up her tempo, leaning back and bracing her hands on Dakota's thighs as she pistoned her hips. Somehow Dakota managed not to grab her and jerk her into her throbbing center. Practiced hands ran higher up Dakota's legs, pressing ever so slightly against the soaked material, nearly setting her off.

"Thirty-second warning," Dakota muttered through clenched teeth. She was about to lose her cool all over the place if she didn't get the hot look in Shawn's eyes out of her head. Shawn. *Fuck!*

Moaning in surrender, Dakota forced her eyes open as she climaxed. She wanted to focus on the blonde in her lap, but all she saw was Shawn.

❖

Shawn nearly went over with Dakota.

She couldn't move, couldn't look away, losing all track of time as she watched the ripples of pleasure course through Dakota's body. As the dancer pushed deeper into Dakota's lap, Shawn's insides twisted each time Dakota stiffened and pushed up out of the chair. Barely breathing, she imagined straddling that tight body, feeling Dakota succumb to pleasure, hearing Dakota cry out her name.

Watching her come in the company of a stranger, she almost forgot her earlier irritation. She squirmed, feeling the effects of Dakota's orgasm to her core. Her hands trembled holding her glass, her throat constricted with every breath. She leaned against the wall when her knees threatened to give way. She could never remember being so turned on as she watched the talented cowgirl satisfy Dakota. Playing the role of voyeur was more exciting than she imagined. Her legs still wouldn't move and her mind went blank as she took in every vivid detail—feeling instead of thinking, watching instead of participating.

She nearly whimpered when Dakota threw her head back and closed her eyes. She wet her lips, focusing on Dakota's breasts, liking the way they pushed against her shirt. Dakota wasn't wearing a bra, and her nipples stood out like two small stones beneath the cotton of her shirt. Shawn's own nipples were rock hard beneath the thin material of her tank top, and her clit throbbed painfully. She covered her mouth with her hand before a cry escaped.

Seeing Dakota in the midst of release was so powerful, Shawn began to regret her decision to shut Dakota out. But what other choice did she have except to say no? Dakota was dangerous for so many reasons. Sure, she was chivalrous, polite, and truly seemed to care about her friends. But she was also cocky and sure of her sex appeal—a strong reminder why playing with her was a bad idea. A lot like playing with fire. Dakota was the unknown, a crapshoot in the game of life. The gallantry tended to be a little annoying, but that part of Dakota's personality was actually starting to grow on her. That was more than a little worrisome. Maybe Dakota's stunt upstairs with the male dancer wasn't a show. Maybe she cared.

And she *had* been relieved when Dakota stepped in and asked the dancer to leave. She even thought when Dakota sat down they could talk, get to know one another…that maybe Dakota could see beyond her looks. Maybe they could even become friends. But then Dakota hit on her and the disappointment stung. She'd briefly lowered her barriers, hoping for more, but she had expected too much. Silly of her to imagine a different outcome, but the disillusionment still hurt. Lesson learned—time to walk away.

But she couldn't.

Shawn was frozen in place even as fire raged through her. She didn't really have any reason to be angry with Dakota. She was the one waffling all over the place, not Dakota, who seemed to be acting true to herself. Dakota protected the people she cared about. Riann had told her as much, and Dakota's actions throughout the night proved she looked after her friends. That trait was pretty damn appealing. As to her flirting with just about any woman that walked by? Not so much, but it really wasn't any of her business. At least with Dakota, she knew where she stood. Her biggest issue was that she couldn't trust herself.

Before she embarrassed herself any further, Shawn pushed her way out into the balmy Vegas night. She had to escape that club, be anywhere but inside that room, watching Dakota so aroused and coming apart in the company of a stranger.

She waited anxiously for a cab, her body still responding to the erotic scene. The pool of wetness between her thighs and the pounding pressure made her grit her teeth. She couldn't deny her attraction to Dakota. She'd be lying to herself. But from what she had just observed, no one else could resist her either. Dancers were paid to excite and tease, but the smile on the dancer's face said she was enjoying her performance a little more than usual. The other dancers looked almost bored when they thought no one was watching them, but the blond cowgirl sliding all over Dakota appeared to have known she had lassoed the huntress. For once Dakota had become the prey.

A taxi driver waved Shawn over just as Dakota rushed out of the club, looking feverish and a little out of breath. Droplets of sweat dotted her skin where her collar fell open, revealing her throat and her rapid pulse. Shawn wanted to place her hand there. Or, better yet, her mouth. When the visions made her clit twitch and her breath catch, she quickly averted her eyes. She had the crazy feeling Dakota would be able to see every image she'd fantasized still burning hotly in her own eyes.

"Hey," Dakota managed to get out. "Can I ride back with you? Terry and Riann want to stay."

Shawn shivered at the huskiness in Dakota's voice. She'd never forget the sexy, melodious tone. A surge of jealousy followed quickly by irritation shot through her. Dakota sounded sexy because some stranger had just made her come in the middle of a sleazy strip club. *Jesus, get a grip!*

"Suit yourself." Shawn hoped her voice sounded controlled as she scooted to the far side of the cab. She tried desperately to hide her fidgeting, but Dakota's scent, heightened by her lingering arousal, didn't make it easy.

They stayed quiet for most of the ride. Shawn focused on the bright neon signs that turned the Vegas night to day and refused to allow Dakota's charms to lure her in, even though she really wanted to press herself against Dakota and lose all sense of time and place. But even though Dakota was all kinds of hot, after her little display inside the club that would never happen.

"So, have you enjoyed Vegas so far?" Dakota asked, her voice steady, the huskiness gone.

After what Shawn had just observed, the line made her laugh. "It's been fine."

"That's it, just fine? What, you don't like men in Speedos?"

"Actually, no, I don't."

Dakota's eyes darkened. "Well, that's reassuring. How about a drink? It's still early."

Unbelievable. Did she ever get enough? That's what Shawn wanted to say, but the last time she declined Dakota's invitation Dakota had ended up in the arms of another woman. Not that she cared. She didn't. Just the same, for half a second she actually considered accepting the offer. She rarely took time off and had only three days to let loose and have fun. But this was also her cousin's best friend, and considering how easily Dakota turned her on and turned her around, Dakota was *not* the type of fun she should dabble in. Besides, she couldn't imagine that only one taste of Dakota would ever satisfy her appetite. Better not to bite in the first place. "I'm tired. Maybe some other time?"

"Sure," Dakota said as the cab lurched to a halt.

"Good night, Dakota."

Shawn jumped out of the cab before she changed her mind. Dakota's disappointed expression thrilled a small part of her. She felt Dakota's eyes on her but never looked back. She needed quiet and sleep, and most of all, she needed to figure out how to handle the rest of the weekend. Dakota was dangerous territory. She'd have to be careful before she stepped out of bounds and did something she'd regret. While every instinct in her screamed that she should turn around and accept Dakota's offer for whatever she had in mind, the sane part of her won. Maybe what happened in Vegas stayed in Vegas, but she just couldn't let anything happen with Dakota, no matter what city she was in. Her decision should have made her happy, but she opened her door feeling as vacant on the inside as the empty room awaiting her.

CHAPTER FIVE

Shawn was exhausted but too wound up to sleep. Images of Dakota getting off on a cheap thrill weren't helping her relax. She walked into the large bathroom, shedding her clothes along the way, and discovered one of her favorite amenities. As soon as she saw the huge oblong Jacuzzi tub, she turned on the taps, her spirits rising.

She couldn't wait to wash away the smell of cigarettes and alcohol from the clubs she'd traipsed through, but more importantly, she wanted to scrub away any memories of the tall, dark-haired woman with a dancer in her lap. She rested her head against the cool tile and closed her eyes, hoping to unwind when a dozen images of Dakota popped up behind her eyelids. So much for forgetting about her. Why did she have to be so damn irresistible?

Staying away from Dakota should have been easy. Shawn was a bartender, used to turning down all types of advances from men and women, but from the minute she'd met Dakota, she'd been taken in by her charm, good looks, and unnerving courtliness. She'd tried avoiding Dakota all evening, shot down all attempts at conversation, and tried to make it perfectly clear she didn't want anything from her. She'd promised herself to avoid women like Dakota after the last disastrous relationship. But damn, she couldn't ignore Dakota's charisma as she cruised the clubs or the sexual pull of her body responding to that dancer. And those eyes…

Shawn stopped doing exactly what she'd resented most from the women she'd dated, who always valued her looks more than anything else. She ended up being a decoration on their arm—a prize to be shown off, but not worthy of a serious relationship. She'd let down her guard when Alex entered her life, and it had taken her a year to pick up the pieces.

Alex had wanted to take care of her too. At first, Shawn considered Alex's possessiveness and jealousy cute, but they quickly became oppressive. Alex didn't treat her like an equal, and the macho-girlfriend act, especially when Alex tried fighting battles Shawn was totally capable of handling on her own, wore on their relationship. Shawn had tried to explain that to Alex one night, but Alex had become so angry she'd lost her temper and almost became physical. That near miss was all the incentive she'd needed to pack her bags.

Burying her past with Alex was one big reason she moved back to Seattle, and she vowed never to be that superficial. Personality would always come before looks, but Dakota had both, and her attractiveness was scary as hell.

Shawn shook her head—she'd just have to deal. She was at her cousin's bachelorette party and she'd have to spend the next few days hanging around with Riann and her friends—including Dakota. Besides, Dakota was more than attractive; she was like flypaper. Shawn couldn't even get close without feeling drawn to her. Everywhere she looked, Dakota was there, flashing that charismatic smile or, worse, being kind and attentive. To top it off, she'd seen what Dakota looked like in stalking mode, had witnessed the predatory glint in her eye. She recalled the way Dakota arched in her chair, remembered the trickle of sweat as it rolled down her neck and disappeared into the opening of her shirt. She'd wanted to chase that droplet with her tongue, to taste its salty essence and continue her quest until she was on her knees in front of Dakota. She'd actually wanted to be the prey, to succumb to the huntress, which was exactly why she shouldn't even think about Dakota. She would never be anyone's trophy again. Her pride wouldn't allow it. And to a woman like Dakota, she would never be more than a temporary trophy.

Now here she was in this beautiful hotel, supposedly to enjoy a stress-free weekend of fun. Instead, she was lying in a bath trying to figure out why she so desperately wanted to sleep with a woman so clearly not good for her.

"Well, that's not going to happen," she muttered, sinking lower into the warm, soapy water, determined to banish Dakota from her mind and body.

The smell of vanilla and peach tickled Shawn's nose as she lathered her breasts, and her nipples hardened. She was still painfully aroused, the heaviness of desire never fully dissipating. She rolled them between her fingertips, throwing her head back as a moan escaped her lips. She was wet, her clit pulsing stronger with each tug of her nipples. She slid lower into the tub and parted her legs, the slightest rush of water pushing against her sensitive folds. She bit her bottom lip and slid her slick fingers between her thighs. As soon as she touched her clitoris, the first warning spasms began. She gasped. What was she doing? She rocketed to a sitting position and squeezed her legs together to stop the impending climax.

Shawn rocked inside the tub, holding her legs close to her chest. She closed her eyes—angry, aroused, confused. She wanted to let go—had wanted to all night. She'd never been with anyone she didn't care about, never had a one-night stand. The concept of "love 'em and leave 'em" had always been foreign to her. But tonight, a big part of her didn't care about all that. She'd actually considered giving in, throwing caution to the wind. But she couldn't. She based her life on caution. Her vigilance was her safety net, even if it meant closing off a piece of herself.

Trembling, she tried to stand, but her legs wouldn't obey. She gripped the sides of the tub, pushing out of the warm water, her nipples hardening further with the sudden drop in temperature.

Ruthlessly ignoring her overstimulated body, she toweled her hair dry, put on a pair of silk pajamas, and sank into bed.

Then she tossed and turned for the next two hours, until the sound of a key card sliding in the lock offered a reprieve. She needed a diversion and could certainly count on Riann and Terry for that. The door banged open and someone cursed.

"Terry?" Shawn called, "you okay?"

"Oh, sorry, Shawn. Tried to be quiet…guess you weren't asleep anyway," Terry mumbled. She stumbled in the dark and fell onto the other bed.

"No problem," Shawn said, wondering at Terry's idea of quiet. She sat up, pulling the sheet with her, and turned on a light. "So, how was the rest of your night?"

Terry, her eyes bloodshot, looked like her Vegas weekend had gotten off to a good start. Her smeared black mascara, messy hair, and the missing top button on her blouse confirmed that suspicion. Yep, another typical night in Vegas.

"Expensive." Terry dragged out the word. "Between the alcohol and the lap dances, I must have blown three hundred bucks. I need to take it easy. We still have two days to go."

"Wow. Well, at least you had fun."

"Yeah." Terry laughed. "I really did. How about you?"

Shawn hesitated. She didn't want to seem ungrateful for Riann's invitation, but the word *fun* wasn't the adjective she would have used.

"Shawn?"

"Oh, sorry. Yeah, it was okay."

"Just okay?" Terry sat on the bed opposite Shawn, gripping the edge of the mattress as if trying not to sway.

"No, really, Terry. I had a good time. I guess I'm just tired from traveling."

"I heard you rode back with Dakota. She didn't upset you, did she?"

Shawn stared at Terry, wondering why one of her friends would immediately conclude that Dakota had done something wrong or inappropriate. Sure, Shawn was upset, but it wasn't Dakota's fault she was having these feelings and didn't know what to do with them. She instinctively felt protective of Dakota and bit back a scowl. "No, she didn't. Why would you ask?"

Terry laughed. "Haven't you been listening all evening? Riann and I know our playgirl friend, and you, my friend, are gorgeous. If you think she won't try to hit on you this weekend, then you're sadly mistaken. Don't get me wrong. I love her like my own sister. Just...don't let your guard down."

Shawn didn't want to hear any of this. She knew how Dakota operated, but that didn't make Terry spelling it out any easier to digest. Instead of thinking or talking about Dakota any longer, she stood and threw the sheets aside. Suddenly she needed some air. "I'll tread carefully, Terry. Thanks for the warning."

"No problem. Hey, where are you off to this late?"

"A walk sounds good. Can't sleep. Will you be awake when I get back?"

Terry heaved herself up and headed to the bathroom. "Doubt it. I sleep like the dead, so don't worry about waking me up."

Shawn dressed quickly and took the elevator down to the casino level. The gaming floor was quiet for the early hour, only a few gamblers scattered at the table and slots. She wasn't much of a gambler and opted for perusing the windows of the hotel gift shop even though she knew it wouldn't be open. Glancing into one of the many bars, she abruptly halted when she saw Dakota sitting at the bar next to a very attractive, very familiar blonde. She was about to make a discreet exit when Dakota locked eyes with her and stood abruptly.

"Shawn, wait!" Dakota yelled over the noise of a slot machine paying off. She said something to the blonde and rapidly cut through the mostly empty tables to Shawn. "Couldn't sleep?"

"No, must be the heat. So, I see you decided to take the blonde up on her *drink* offer," Shawn said, nodding with her chin toward the bar. She shouldn't have said anything, but the words tumbled out before she could stop them. She studied Dakota, who resembled a bobber sitting on the surface of the water, waiting for the first woman willing to take a bite and submerge her. First the bar dancer hooked her. Then Dakota tried to get Shawn to nibble in the cab. Now the woman who had asked Dakota to share a cab at the airport was sitting at the bar. By the way the blonde's eyes never strayed from Dakota, she was obviously ready and waiting to jump on the bait.

If Shawn's question surprised Dakota, she didn't show it. "Her name is Christine and, yes, we're having a drink. Is there a problem?"

"No, none at all. I hope you two have fun. Sorry to interrupt." Shawn tried for a quick exit. The problem was all hers.

"Shawn, wait. Please wait." Dakota gently grasped Shawn's arm. "I'll say good-bye to her if you'll just…please stay?"

Shawn eased her arm free from Dakota's grip, but the pleading look on Dakota's face caught her off guard. Dakota wanted to spend time with her, and she might as well admit she felt the same. "All right."

"Great," Dakota said. "Don't move. I'll be right back."

Shawn could tell by the blonde's body language she didn't appreciate receiving the brush-off. Secretly pleased that Dakota had chosen to be with her instead, she kept her expression neutral. No need to gloat, and besides, she didn't want to give Dakota the wrong impression. She wanted to get to know Riann's friend— not date her.

When Dakota returned, she guided Shawn through the nearly empty bar, gesturing for her to take a seat at one of the many private booths.

"Why are you up so late?" Shawn asked as Dakota slid into the booth across from her.

"The heat. It gives me headaches."

Shawn remembered Dakota swallowing some aspirin earlier

and winced. "The music in the clubs must have been killing you."

"I got used to it."

"Good to hear," Shawn said dryly, surprised that after the lap dance Dakota's brain had any blood flowing to it at all.

"Can I get you a drink...something to eat?" Dakota asked.

"No, nothing, thank you. I'm too tired to eat and I don't drink."

"I noticed. Was that just tonight or all the time?"

Shawn needed to make a decision. She could either walk away or continue a conversation that was heading into personal territory. She'd already decided to keep her distance, but their first moments of being alone, with Dakota's attention solely focused on her, were pleasant enough to keep her firmly in her seat.

"I don't drink because I'm a bartender and I see what alcohol can do to people when consumed in large quantities."

"Is that the only reason?"

Shawn focused on the blue-lit bar behind Dakota but didn't see the bar. She saw her father, heard his angry voice. She didn't want to say any more, but Dakota's deep voice was so soothing and caring she kept going. Her hands trembled where they rested on her thighs. "No, it's not the only reason."

"Shawn?"

Dakota's obvious sincerity was too much for Shawn. She could handle the aggressive, overbearing Dakota, but the one sitting before her wasn't the same person she'd witnessed earlier in the club. This gentle, attentive Dakota wasn't looking at her as just another conquest. This one was the most dangerous of all. Shawn's emotions were running high, she was exhausted, and remembering her father's constant drunken state made tears touch the corners of her eyes. To her horror, they fell.

Dakota reached across the table and intertwined her fingers with Shawn's. There was nothing sexual in the touch, but Shawn felt the electricity down to her toes. She should have pulled away but couldn't.

"Shawn…please. Tell me what's wrong?" Dakota rubbed her thumb over the back of Shawn's hand.

That thumb was playing havoc on Shawn's system. She slowly disentangled their hands, feeling the loss instantly. "Nothing much to tell. Nothing worth talking about anyway."

"I understand, but are you all right?"

"Yes, I'm fine. It's just…my father is an alcoholic. I'm not fond of the topic."

"Oh, Shawn, I'm sorry. I didn't mean to bring up a painful subject."

"You couldn't know, now, could you?" Shawn wanted to steer clear of any more revelations, especially when she noticed the empathy in Dakota's dark brown eyes. Understanding and… pain. The idea of Dakota hurting bothered her. "No need to apologize. It's not your fault."

"I understand that, but it's not your fault either. Still, it must be hard for you."

"That's nice of you to say, but I'm not so sure about the first part."

"Would you like to talk about it?"

"No, but thanks for the offer. I should go back to my room. It's getting late and I have a feeling that if we're late for anything tomorrow, Terry will be a nightmare."

"You have her pegged." Dakota paused, the intense focus back in her eyes. "Can I walk you there?"

Shawn wanted to say yes but reined in her emotions before they got the best of her. She appreciated Dakota listening to her. Not too many people in her life had ever taken the time to get to know her. But that was where her appreciation needed to end. "No, I'll be fine. Good night, Dakota."

"Good night, then." Dakota stood and shoved her hands into the pockets of her jeans but made no move to follow her. "I'll see you tomorrow?"

"I guess you will." Shawn smiled and Dakota returned the smile. That small gesture combined with Dakota's hands clearly twitching in her pockets made Shawn's heart soar. She liked the idea that she made the confident and sure Dakota nervous, and for the first time since arriving in Vegas, she headed back to her room looking forward to the next few days.

CHAPTER SIX

*T*he smoke was thick, choking. Dakota's lungs burned, and her chest felt as tight as if a thousand-pound weight pinned her down. Flames soared around her, hungrily devouring everything in their path. The desperate need to reach her destination mounted. She struggled with every step, the walls crashing around her like falling trees. Seconds remained until the house would be swallowed up along with everything she loved.

She clawed her way upstairs, making it down the long, narrow hallway to within inches of the wooden door. She gripped the gold knob. Pain seared her palm. The superheated metal scorched her hand, instantly forming blisters. She pushed past the pain, biting down so hard on her lip that blood dripped onto the white of her T-shirt. She thought she heard herself scream, but no sound emerged from her throat. She twisted the knob, her tortured flesh tearing.

Locked.

"Mom...Dad..." She choked, coughed, desperate to expel the dark smoke that filled her lungs. She covered her mouth with her sleeve and kicked the handle of her parents' bedroom door. Nothing moved.

The smoke was an impenetrable wall. Her eyes burned and the pressure inside her chest prevented her from sucking in a breath. Holding in what air she had left, she kicked again. She *needed to get through the door—just one more second, and the nightmare would be over.*

Please...please...open.

Using the last of her strength, she slammed her shoulder into the door. Wood splintered. Relief poured through her. She pushed aside the only barrier that separated her from her family and forced her way into the room. A wave of heat struck her like a fist and a bright flash of light burst in front of her eyes. A giant blast blew her backward, knocking her to the floor. She covered her face with her hands, trying to shield herself from the intense heat. Dizzy and disoriented, she staggered back to her feet. She managed to take one more unsteady step forward but was too late.

The floor to her parents' room caved in. She watched in horror as flames engulfed her family.

"No!"

"Dakota, wake up, wake up!" A voice nagged her from somewhere in the distance.

Dakota shot straight up in bed, glancing with confusion around the room. The sheets beneath her hand were soaked through with sweat. She was shaking. *Damn, not again.*

"Honey, you okay?" Riann's cool hand settled on her cheek.

"Yeah, I'm fine."

"Says who?" Riann jammed her hand on her hip and shot Dakota *the look.*

Uh-oh. Dakota shook the cobwebs out of her brain. Riann was wrapped in a towel and her hair was wet, evidence that she had just stepped out of the shower. "Uh..."

"When did they start again?"

Pushing her hands through her damp hair, Dakota swung her legs over the edge of the bed. "When did *what* start again?"

"Really? You're going to pull that shit with me?"

"What *shit* are you referring to?" Dakota looked away from Riann, willing her pulse to slow.

"Dakota!"

"All right, all right. Not very long ago. Forget it. I'm fine now."

Dakota tried to rise, but Riann caught her by the shoulder. "Damn it. How many times do we have to go through this? I care how you feel, honey, but I can't help you if you don't let me in."

Dakota managed to make it to her feet, dislodging Riann's hand. Riann was only trying to help, but Dakota needed space. She dropped onto the couch and covered her eyes with her arm. "I have nightmares sometimes—it's no big deal. I used to have them when I was younger too, and you didn't grill me about them then. So just...leave it alone."

"All right, if that's what you want. You need to get dressed. We're late."

"Oh, shit! Is everyone here?" Dakota jumped up. "Terry's going to filet me, isn't she?"

"Possibly." Riann grinned. "Everyone's been here since seven. Terry called the room about a half hour ago wanting to storm up here and 'drag your lazy ass out of bed.' I told her we were on our way down."

Dakota grabbed a pair of black pants and a short-sleeved white T-shirt from her open suitcase in the corner and pulled them on. She quickly slipped on her black boots and finger-combed her hair. "Thanks for covering for me. Let me brush my teeth and I'll be all set."

"I don't know how the hell you do that."

"Do what?" Dakota smiled innocently.

"Nothing! That's exactly my point. It takes me two hours to dress and get my hair right, and even then, it never looks as good as yours. It's just wrong."

Dakota pulled her hair back into a ponytail, securing it with a Southwestern-colored hair tie. "It's genetics, sweetie."

"Huh." Riann pretended to pout.

Dakota headed for the bathroom to splash cold water on her face. Time to face Terry. Her stomach quivered. And say good morning to Shawn.

❖

Dakota and Riann stepped out of the elevator and headed to the lobby. Dakota waved to the rest of Riann's party, who were checking in at the registration desk. The twelve women were eagerly chatting about the upcoming weekend, and she ought to go say hi, but she just wanted to find Shawn. Once Terry got hold of them, she wouldn't have a second to talk to her. Terry was nowhere in sight. Maybe she had a few minutes…

"Dakota?"

Dakota grimaced as someone tapped her on the shoulder from behind. Ah, *there* she was. "Hi, Terry."

"Glad you two could join us this morning. Here." Terry shoved a new list of activities into Dakota's hand. "Just in case you lost the *first* copy."

"Sorry." Dakota slid behind Riann, trying to get out of the line of fire.

Riann reached behind her and grabbed Dakota by the arm. She yanked hard, forcing Dakota closer so that she could whisper into her ear. "You're such a chickenshit. Come out from behind me and take your medicine like a good girl."

"Thanks for the support," Dakota muttered. Rocking back and forth on her heels, she shot Terry her "charming" smile. "Sorry I made Riann late."

"That Riley charm won't work on me." Terry tried not to smile but Dakota saw through her. "You owe me a drink later—a really big one."

"You're on," Dakota said, thankful Terry didn't rip into her in front of everyone. Most of the time she wouldn't have been concerned, but she didn't want anyone to talk down to her in front of Shawn. She looked over the group. No Shawn. "So, ah, is everyone here?"

"Yep…well, everyone except Shawn. She wasn't feeling well this morning, so I told her to relax and we'd meet her at the room."

Dakota shoved her hands into her pockets in an attempt to hide her anxiety. Shawn not feeling well didn't make sense. She'd been fine when they parted last night. Even though they didn't seem to click well at first, they'd found some sort of truce after spending a few uninterrupted moments together. The thought of something being wrong with Shawn made her ache, and not in a good way. She was ready to suggest that they go check on Shawn when a familiar form appeared, escalating her blood pressure into the stratosphere. Missy Ruffington.

"Dakota…stop that," Terry said quietly, elbowing Dakota in the ribs when she heard the familiar low growl.

"Ugh." Dakota winced when the shot sank perfectly into her side. "Damn, for a moment I forgot she was coming."

"She's been here since seven. Supposedly she had to powder her nose."

Dakota leaned forward and whispered, "No matter how much powder she uses, it'll never be enough."

Terry disguised her laughter by coughing into her hand just as Missy strode up to Riann, placing fake kisses on both sides of her face.

Dakota leaned against the check-in counter. She didn't want to get into anything with Missy. She wanted to check on Shawn, and as soon as Terry moved everyone on to point two on the day's list, she could.

Missy took her time making her rounds, giving everyone in the group a hug or an air-kiss before finally ending up in front of Dakota. Dakota detested that fake-kissing crap. She also understood that her distaste for Missy was mutual.

"Dakota, *darling*, how nice to see you again."

Missy didn't just speak. She purred, dragging out each

word longer than necessary. The catlike tone was as annoying as someone running their nails down a chalkboard. Dakota plastered on a smile. Just make nice. Make nice and it will be all over. "I'm surprised you could join us, Missy. I know how busy you are."

"I've been very busy, but never too busy for friends. Besides, I *am* looking forward to this weekend. The strip clubs, the shopping, and all the gorgeous men. How could anyone have a bad time in Vegas? Oh, but I forgot. None of that is your *thing*, is it, Dakota?" Missy smiled sweetly. Sweet like saccharin was sweet, with a bite underneath. "Well, I'm sure you'll find something to occupy your time. Maybe a nice massage?"

Dakota leaned against the counter and swallowed a comeback. She refused to allow Missy to get to her. This weekend was about Riann, not her. But man, not killing Missy would take work.

"I'm sure we'll *all* have fun this weekend, but more importantly, I know *Riann* is looking forward to it."

"Oh, Dakota, always so serious. Riann *will* have a great time. *I'll* make sure of it."

Dakota clenched her teeth. Restraint definitely wasn't one of her strong suits. She was teetering on the edge of saying something that she'd most likely regret when she saw an athletic blonde headed her way. Saved! Dakota pushed away from the counter and grabbed her in a bear hug.

"Coal! Wow, you look gorgeous." Dakota kissed the shorter woman's cheek.

"Thanks. You're looking pretty good yourself. I see you're getting along with everyone," Coal said, trying to break free of Dakota's hug with no success.

"Yeah, thanks for the rescue. Wanna ditch this crowd with me for a while?" she whispered, making Coal laugh.

"Oh, Dakota, always the charmer."

"Well, you know me. I'm a sucker for—"

"You better unhand my wife," a familiar deep voice warned from behind Dakota, "before I beat you uglier than you are now."

Grinning, Dakota pivoted, keeping Coal in her arms as she met her cousin's dark eyes. "Come on, Jay, when did you lose your sense of humor?"

"The moment those lips touched my wife's face," Jay said. "I can only imagine where they've been since you've been here."

She wanted to say "no, you can't," as surprised as Jay would be at her lack of action so far. Her cousin Jay was as close to her as a sister, and when she'd asked Riann to include Jay and her new wife in the bachelorette party, Riann had readily agreed. Riann had taken to Coal right away. Figured. Coal had the same fiery personality as Riann.

"Girls, play nice." Coal slipped from underneath Dakota's arms and into Jay's, then threaded her hand through Jay's dark hair and pulled her down for a welcoming kiss. "You have nothing to worry about, darling. The only kiss I want is yours."

Dakota stared at the two lovers, wondering if marriage and that kind of love could ever be possible for someone like her. The thought almost made her jerk back in shock and she laughed to cover her surprise. "Well, after that little show, I guess I shouldn't ask how sex after marriage is?"

"The sex is amazing, as always," Jay said with a touch of cockiness. "Thanks for asking, cuz. I guess I don't have to ask how your playgirl ass is holding up in the sex department. Especially in a town like Vegas."

"Maybe I'll fill you in later, cousin. Although now that you're married, I don't know if your heart could take it." Dakota enjoyed teasing her but hoped Jay didn't recognize the familiar ploy to steer the conversation away from herself. She wasn't ready to admit she hadn't been playing with anyone, especially not when Jay knew her so well. The lap dance didn't exactly count. That had all been about Shawn, and she didn't know how to process the unusual feelings she was having for her. She'd already scoured the lobby every few seconds hoping she'd appear. She'd never had a woman consume her every thought before. It was irritating. Irritating, and confusing.

"Okay, you two, that's enough," Coal said. "Public place here."

"Okay, babe," Jay said seriously.

"Ah, domestication. Gotta love it." Dakota threw an arm around Jay's shoulder, letting her know the teasing was all in fun. She appreciated how much marriage meant to Jay, even though she couldn't imagine marrying anyone. That amount of trust, that amount of dependence would be far too much. Sadness hit her unexpectedly, the pain so acute it was like ripping open an old wound. Loneliness swamped her and she shuddered. Maybe the sadness came from knowing Jay had found such happiness in settling down but that she never would—maybe.

Jay gestured to the rest of the party and the piles of luggage surrounding them. "Hey, D, what do you say we help these ladies with their luggage. Then we can find some place to do a little sparring. God knows I haven't given you a good ass kickin' in a long time."

"Sounds good," Dakota said. Anything to occupy her mind and work off this funk. Anything to stop thinking crazy thoughts about Shawn.

❖

Shawn couldn't believe how many people were crammed into the room she shared with Terry. Luggage was everywhere. The only available space was in front of the buffet table that had been set up under a window overlooking the Vegas skyline.

She didn't know any of the new arrivals and looked anxiously for Dakota, but she hadn't come in with the rest of the group. Feeling a little overwhelmed, she was about to slip into the hall when Dakota walked in, followed by two other striking women. Dakota looked better than she remembered in the same tight black jeans and black boots she'd worn at the airport. Her hair was pulled back in a ponytail and her dark eyes scanned the room as if she had a singular goal in mind. For a split second, Shawn hoped she was the object of Dakota's search. When their eyes locked, Shawn's heart raced and she nearly stumbled. Dakota smiled, the small gesture tilting Shawn's upended world back onto its axis. Most women probably welcomed the thrill of being on the receiving end of a smile like that, but Shawn knew the downside. Thrilling today, heartbreaking tomorrow. Nope. Not again. She quickly turned away and headed for the buffet. She grabbed a plate and joined the crowd in line, making it as far as the fruit when a familiar scent caught her attention. Sandalwood and spice. Her knees shook.

"How are you feeling?" Dakota asked.

"What do you mean?"

"Terry said you weren't feeling well. I just wanted to make sure you were all right."

Shawn found the concerned overture safe enough. They could have a friendly adult conversation, couldn't they? "Just a headache. I feel much better than I did an hour ago. Thanks."

"Well, as you know, I'm the expert on headaches. But since you're feeling better, can I get you some juice or something?"

Shawn ought to point out she was capable of picking up breakfast items without help, but the concern in Dakota's voice and the worry in her eyes stopped her. Dakota's face was very expressive, something she remembered vividly from watching her with a dancer in her lap.

Suddenly that same image that had aroused her mere hours ago made her irritable. She couldn't blame Dakota for enjoying her weekend like everyone else, but *she* wasn't just anyone else. "I'm fine. Riann's waving me over. Excuse me."

"Okay," Dakota said. "Sure. Look, maybe later—"

"Things will probably be pretty crazy." Shawn backed away. "Have fun this weekend."

Shawn fled before she got caught in Dakota's spell.

❖

Dakota absently snacked on an apple, confused by Shawn's ever-changing behavior. She'd only wanted to make sure Shawn was all right, but her friendly attempt had somehow backfired. She questioned her motives, but her behavior seemed no different than if one of her other friends had suddenly become ill. Okay, maybe that really wasn't true. Her reaction had been different. Hearing that Shawn was alone and possibly sick had torn at her insides. That response made no sense—she couldn't even consider Shawn a friend yet, though the thought made for a nice possibility, especially after their talk last night. All the same, when she had abruptly walked away, Dakota wanted to beg her to stay. She didn't, of course. No way would she beg someone to spend time with her. Ever.

Dakota tossed her apple core as Riann got pulled away by some of her party. Personal issues aside, Shawn was alone and a newcomer. She had to be feeling uncomfortable. Dakota grabbed two juices and headed across the room.

"Here," she said, handing Shawn a glass. "I thought you'd like a refill."

"Thank you. That was very sweet."

"Yeah…well…" Man, she'd have to stop letting Shawn get to her like this. One compliment and she became a steaming pile of mush. "Would you like me to introduce you to some of Riann's friends?" A tiny prick of gratification stole through her when a look of relief crossed Shawn's face.

"I'm sure I'll have time to meet them all eventually, but who's that tall woman surrounded by the crowd of women?"

"*That* would be Missy Ruffington," Dakota said, having a hard time keeping the disdain out of her voice.

"And may I ask why you don't like her?"

"How do you know that?"

Shawn smiled. "To be honest, you're very easy to read. I've had some practice after all my years of working in a bar."

Could Shawn have said anything worse? She didn't want to

be easy to read. She was a private person and couldn't let anyone know some things about her. "Is that so?"

Shawn nodded just as Terry called out, making all the women in the room nearly stand at attention.

"Ladies, it's time to take a walk down the strip. You have less than an hour to freshen up, then grab your purses and pull out your credit cards. It's time to shop Vegas style!"

"She's like a general commanding her troops," Shawn commented as cheers of "shop, shop, shop" emanated inside the room.

"Yeah, and we better fall into step before we get court-martialed," Dakota said, making Shawn laugh. "I'll see you in about an hour?"

"Sure. Where are you off to before the big shopping trip?"

"My cousin, Jay, wants me to sneak off with her for a few minutes to do a little sparring in one of the empty conference rooms."

"Sparring?"

"Yeah, you know…martial-arts stuff."

"Are you some kind of black belt or something?"

"Actually, yes, but I don't teach or anything."

"You won't get hurt, will you?"

The tinge of worry in Shawn's voice made Dakota's heart soar. Except for Riann's occasional sisterly concern, she hadn't had someone worry about her in a long time. Even if it was only a smidgeon of worry, something Shawn might have felt for anyone, she'd take it. "No, I'll be fine. I usually end up kicking my cousin's butt within a few minutes, so not to worry."

Jay walked up and threw her arm around Dakota's shoulder. "You wish."

"And I assume this is your cousin?" Shawn asked, and laughed.

"Jay DiAngelo—Shawn Camello," Dakota said.

"Ooh, an Italian woman," Jay said teasingly, wiggling her

eyebrows. "Well, it's nice to meet you, Shawn. I'd introduce you to my wife but she's talking wedding stuff with Riann. So, what is this I overheard about you kicking my butt?"

"I was just telling Shawn that you probably won't last more than two minutes before I drop you."

"We'll see, cuz. We'll see. Good meeting you, Shawn. I need to tell my wife Dakota and I are sneaking off before she thinks she lost me for the weekend. Don't want to be sleeping on the couch."

"You're so whipped," Dakota said, punching Jay's arm playfully.

"I know, but I love it."

Dakota grinned as Jay disappeared and caught Shawn smiling faintly at her. She shrugged self-consciously. "What?"

"Nothing. I can tell you love each other. It's kinda cute."

To Dakota's horror, she felt herself blush. She never blushed—ever. "Yeah...okay...well...I'll see you in about an hour."

"Dakota?" Shawn grasped Dakota's arm. "Be careful, okay?"

"Of course."

Dakota stared at the soft hand wrapped around her bicep. Shawn's smooth skin was so warm she didn't want her to let go. Shawn had thrown her off balance again, but for the first time, having a woman knock the breath out of her was kind of appealing. If the woman was Shawn.

❖

Dakota pivoted as a sweeping hook kick rocketed toward her head, blocking with her forearm. She didn't get her block up fast enough and Jay's heel caught the edge of her jaw, dropping her like a rock.

"Dakota, can you hear me? Dakota!"

Dakota shook the cobwebs out of her brain and moved to a

seated position. "Nice kick." She wiggled her jaw from side to side, making sure that it was operating properly. "I guess I'm a little rusty."

"No, you were just never that good," Jay countered, patting her affectionately on the leg.

"Oh, really?" Dakota moved quickly, grabbing Jay by her shirt. She flipped Jay over onto her back, pinning her until she conceded defeat with a tap out. "What was that?"

Jay grunted. "Damn you! You weren't hurt at all, were you?"

Dakota rolled off her, propping herself up onto her elbows. "Only stunned for a moment. You know better than to let your guard down like that. What happened?"

"What do you mean, what happened?"

"I mean what happened? It's not that difficult a question. When we were kids, you would have pointed out to everyone within earshot how you kicked my ass whether I was unconscious or not." Dakota couldn't decipher the enigmatic look that covered Jay's face. Seconds later, a smile replaced the look.

"Coal happened."

When Jay spoke, her words were soft, and the calmness in her voice surprised Dakota as much as the statement. "Excuse me?"

"Coal happened," Jay repeated. "She's changed my life."

"Cousin, I'm not following you."

"What's not to understand? I fell in love. Head over heels, no thought necessary—forever love. I haven't been the same since."

Dakota stared at Jay, not comprehending what any of that had to do with their recent sparring match. "Let me paraphrase. You getting your butt kicked by me just now happened because you fell in *love*?"

"Exactly. But I wouldn't say I was the one who got my butt *kicked*."

Dakota chuckled heartily. "Okay, I'll have to agree. That

shot to the face was textbook. I see those long legs of yours are still dangerous."

"I use what I got."

"So I've heard." Dakota removed her gloves and threw them into Jay's bag. "So, are you planning to tell me what you meant?"

Jay threw her head back against the wall and exhaled, a familiar gesture that meant whatever she was about to say would be serious. "I don't know if you'll understand, cuz."

"Try me."

"For a long time I could have anyone I wanted, but I was always lonely. Something was missing, but I couldn't put my finger on it. Women were just for sex, nothing more. Then Coal appeared. She's beautiful, sexy, and so damn determined. She made me see life in a whole new way, and every time we were together, my life felt complete. The day I met her she had me in a tailspin and I've been hooked ever since. She understands me, Dakota—in here." Jay tapped two fingers over her heart. "In places no one has ever touched before."

Dakota listened intently, the words striking a surprisingly familiar chord. Shawn was doing the same thing to her, making her think about things she'd never wanted or even contemplated before that weekend. She'd been focused on Shawn the entire time they'd been sparring. That was why Jay's foot had connected with her face. She wouldn't tell her all this, though. Jay knew her too well and would ask too many probing questions. She wasn't ready to discuss Shawn, not until she had a better handle on the situation. "That's it? So let me summarize. She's great between the sheets, she knows what kind of toothpaste you like, and she can manipulate you into doing whatever she wants, and that made you want to marry her?"

Jay let out a hearty laugh. "Why did I even try? You weren't listening to me at all."

Oh, yeah. She'd heard every word. She just didn't understand it all yet. Maybe Jay could unknowingly help fill in some blanks.

"I was listening. Just answer this. How can you be happy with one person with so many women out there? Not that I'm not *overwhelmingly* happy for you, but how did you know Coal was the one?"

Dakota had never contemplated settling down until twenty-four hours ago. No woman had ever sparked that kind of interest. This was ridiculous. She couldn't be seriously thinking about Shawn as "the one." Settling down meant commitment and commitment equaled falling in love. Falling in love meant that she'd have to give her heart away, and matters of the heart usually ended painfully.

"She just is for me. And when you find the right person one day, everything will make sense."

"Since when did you get all Zen on me?" Dakota ducked when Jay tried to whack her over the head with one of her gloves.

"When you started asking me all these serious questions. Something on your mind you want to discuss?"

"No. But I'd appreciate it if you keep that offer open." Dakota held out a hand, helping Jay off the ground. The way her weekend was progressing, she might need to revisit their conversation sooner rather than later.

CHAPTER SEVEN

"That was so much fun." Shawn pushed her way through the turnstile at the New York-New York roller coaster, still coming off the high of the exciting ride. Dakota wasn't far behind.

"Yeah, that was great. I don't think Terry liked it, though." Dakota pointed to a hunched-over Terry puking into a nearby garbage can.

"Poor Terry. Should we do something?"

"Like what? She's probably still getting over last night's hangover, and I doubt that roller coaster was a good remedy."

"You're probably right."

"Probably?" Dakota wiggled her eyebrows and Shawn gave her a playful shove.

"Stop," Shawn said. "I feel terrible having so much fun when Terry's so sick."

"Yeah, you're right. Hey," Dakota called over the crowd to Riann, who held Terry's hair away from her face. "What's next?"

"We're going to try for manicures before lunch at one."

"Manicures, right." Grumbling, Dakota led the group in the direction of the Bellagio Hotel.

Crowds lined the busy strip as the group made the two-block trip in the 105-degree heat. Anyone who'd ever visited Vegas knew two blocks equaled at least a half-hour walk. Shawn was taking the weather in stride, but as she glanced at Dakota, the undeniably rigid posture and the way she roughly swiped the perspiration off her forehead suggested she wasn't enjoying the temperature at all.

Shawn lingered in the gardens inside the Bellagio while one of Riann's friends tried to schedule last-minute manicures with the concierge. The flowers were an array of colors and beautiful patterns, but she concentrated on Dakota leaning over her shoulder from behind.

"What's the matter," Dakota said, taking a seat with her on a bench under an arbor, "passing on the beauty treatment?"

"I thought I'd sightsee instead."

"I don't suppose you want company? We could catch the dancing-water show in a few minutes."

She should say no and keep her promise to herself to stay away from Dakota, but she really didn't want to see the beautiful show alone. And Dakota looked so hopeful, and harmless, right now. "Okay."

"Great." Dakota smiled and Shawn's heart did a little dance. Oh, this was bad.

They took their time gazing out over the strip, ogling the incredible facades of the grand hotels while being shameless gawking tourists. Shawn couldn't remember a more enjoyable time. Vegas was exciting, but her pleasure wasn't due to the glitter and glitz. Her enjoyment had everything to do with the person standing next to her, who made the day fly past in a blur of excitement and nervous anticipation. Dakota rarely left her side, and every time they brushed against one another, Shawn's pulse raced and her thighs vibrated with tension.

When the enormous pool in front of the Bellagio sprang to life and arcs of water danced to the famous Gene Kelly tune, "Singin' in the Rain," Shawn sang along. She'd loved that movie, probably because her mother loved it too.

"That's quite a smile you're sporting," Dakota said.

"The song makes me think about my mom."

"Does she like this song too?"

"She did." Shawn looked away.

"Oh, Shawn, I'm sorry." Dakota stroked her arm. "I didn't know."

"It's okay. They're good memories. She loved that old movie and the rain. Probably one of the reasons she never wanted to leave Seattle to move to Chicago."

"I love it too," Dakota said. "Always have."

"The rain or Seattle?"

"Both. Have you enjoyed your move back?"

"Oh, yeah. Absolutely. I love Seattle. The climate, the trees, all that fresh air. How could anyone not like it?"

"I'd have to agree with you there." Dakota scooted closer as the music ended and the waters misted back into the pool. "Did you like the water show?"

"It was incredible." Shawn looked away from the water and into Dakota's eyes. How could anyone's eyes be so dark, so welcoming? "What?"

"I knew you'd like it."

"Did you now?"

"Yep."

"How?"

Dakota placed her hand on the railing, her fingers brushing Shawn's hand. She leaned closer, kissing close. "I don't know. I just…knew."

"I thought you said you were going to be careful." Shawn ran her thumb below the small bruise that had formed under Dakota's left eye. "Did you get punched?"

"Kicked," Dakota replied thickly.

Shawn shivered at the huskiness in Dakota's voice. The hazy look in her eyes was mesmerizing—and familiar. She'd seen the same gaze only yesterday, but then it had been fixed on a dancer. The cloudy, lost look was enough to remind her that they needed to go. "Thank you for showing me that. We should get back before the group misses us."

Dakota mumbled something as they walked back inside, but the wall of noise that greeted them as they reentered the casino drowned the words out. "What was that?"

"Uh…I said, what have you enjoyed most about Vegas so far?"

"The water show. But I'm really looking forward to Mystère tonight. How about you?"

"I really don't have a favorite. I like Vegas in general because it's a sexy town. I just hate the heat."

Shawn could think of a lot of adjectives to describe Vegas, but sexy wasn't one of them. "Sexy? I was thinking loud and smoky, but please continue."

"Well, how could it not be? For instance, see that cocktail waitress over there?"

Shawn nodded. How could she miss her? Black lace stockings sheathing long legs. A low-cut blouse leaving little to the imagination. "Yes."

"That's just it. Where else do you see people dressed like that for work? Half-naked females are everywhere you look—dancers, strippers, women walking the streets offering a good time. Nowhere else in the world can you smell, see, and taste sex twenty-four seven. To me that's incredible."

Shawn really was starting to understand, but probably not in the way Dakota would have liked. Unintentionally, Dakota had just given her a unique glimpse into her personality, and unfamiliar pangs of jealousy shot through her. She didn't like being jealous in general—the emotion was petty. She liked even less being jealous of a woman who had every right to enjoy sex however she wanted.

"Drink?" the tall brunette asked.

"No, not for me. Shawn—"

"No, thank you. I'm going back to my room to lie down. Can I take a rain check?" Shawn smiled weakly and avoided looking at Dakota.

"Yeah, of course. Sure. Are you okay?"

"Yeah, I'm fine. Just tired. Thanks." She made her way through the maze of squealing machines and cigarette smoke to the elevator, depressed at the knowledge she had been totally right about Dakota. Dakota was a player, and she refused to get played.

❖

Dakota waited with the rest of the group inside the bar at the Rainforest Café. She tried to strike up a conversation with Shawn, but she always seemed to be busy talking with someone else. Thanks to Terry's planning, they took their seats not long after arriving, a coup by Vegas standards. Dakota grabbed a seat next to Shawn. She still didn't understand why Shawn had abandoned her at the Bellagio, but she was determined to reconnect.

"What are you going to have?" she asked casually, trying hard to ignore the way Shawn's tank top clung to her breasts. Of course, she could stare at any part of Shawn for hours, but it bothered her that a guy sitting at an adjacent table was ogling Shawn like a kid would a new bike. She bit back a scowl. The last time she'd tried to intercept a guy with his sights on Shawn hadn't worked out so well. "Dakota?"

"I'm sorry?"

"I *said*, I'm really not sure, but everything looks great. How about you?"

"I think I'll have the burger and fries." Dakota set her menu aside and watched Shawn chew nervously on her lower lip, an adorable trait, but Dakota was more concerned about what troubled her about the menu. She followed Shawn's gaze, to the prices listed vertically on the far right side. This problem she could solve. "But I should have the lobster, considering this meal is on Terry."

"Well, it's a good thing lobster isn't on the menu, isn't it?" Terry chided her, pointing at her margarita glass for Dakota to fill. "Thanks."

"I'm surprised you could drink so soon after your little display this morning," Dakota said, making everyone laugh.

"Do you *really* want me to discuss your particular displays of excess this weekend, my friend? Let's see," Terry said, extending a finger. "One, the concierge when we arrived. Two, the woman in the cab. Three—"

"Okay, okay." Dakota held up her hand. "I apologize and you're right. Let me pour you a drink." She'd never felt the need to defend her actions. But she'd also never cared about what anyone else thought of her choices. Pouring a new round for the table, she stopped when she reached Shawn. "Can I get you something else besides water?"

"No, thank you. Water's fine," Shawn said, keeping her attention glued to the menu.

Dakota set down the pitcher, at a loss for words. Being one step behind all the time was driving her crazy. She was always in control when it came to women, mostly because the women she chose to date seemed to prefer it that way. Shawn was a completely new experience and Dakota was off her game. She needed to find a way to get back on track soon before this roller coaster of a weekend completely derailed her.

❖

Nothing about the weekend was turning out as Shawn had expected. She'd anticipated some sightseeing, a little shopping, and spending some time with Riann's friends. Women had not figured into her equation, especially not a woman she didn't want to be attracted to and couldn't seem to avoid.

Ignoring Dakota at the table while everyone else talked amongst themselves was just plain rude, though, and Dakota didn't deserve that. As Shawn picked at her salad, she searched for a safe topic. Dakota's obvious discomfort appeared to be a good place to start.

"Is this trip really painful for you?" Shawn murmured.

Dakota ducked her head and grinned. "You can tell?"

"A little. Are you having fun at all?"

"Actually, I enjoyed watching the water show with you a lot."

"Really?" Shawn studied Dakota in an attempt to decipher if she was telling the truth.

"Sure. You act surprised."

Maybe because she was surprised. Shawn desperately wanted to believe Dakota because this was what she craved: someone to listen to her, someone who cared about her thoughts—her likes and dislikes. Dakota's admission combined with her gentle expression made Shawn's throat tighten. "I liked spending time with you too. But the roller coaster was my favorite."

"You mean you didn't enjoy the gardens?"

"Of course I did. They were beautiful. But the adrenaline rush from that roller coaster was insane."

"I'd never have pegged you as an adrenaline junkie."

"Junkie's a strong word. Let's just say I like new and exciting things."

"Really? Like?"

The darkening of Dakota's eyes clued Shawn in that she needed to change the direction of their conversation. She needed to remember to be light and simple. "So why do you think I'd like the gardens more?"

If Dakota was surprised by the sudden shift in conversation she didn't show it.

"I guess because I watched you today," Dakota said. "I don't know. You looked…content there. Like you belonged."

"You watched me?"

Dakota shrugged. "Well, not like a stalker or anything."

"Dakota, I'm messing with you. Relax. What did you notice?"

"You spent a lot of time gazing at the roses. Are they your favorite?"

"Yes. They were my mother's favorite too." Shawn paused.

.What was wrong with her? That was the second time she'd mentioned her mom today. Dakota squeezing her hand under the table brought her back to the present. "Sorry."

"It's okay," Dakota whispered.

"Is it?" God, how she wanted it to be. Her life had never seemed the same after her mom died.

"Yeah. It is. Back to the roses. What was your favorite display?"

Shawn returned the squeeze, not relinquishing Dakota's hand, her own silent thank-you for the change in subject. "The American flag made of all the different types. The artwork was incredible."

"I thought so too. My dad would have really liked it."

This was the opening Shawn had been waiting for. Dakota was a great listener, but Shawn didn't know the first thing about her, other than the whole playgirl thing. Even now, when Dakota mentioned her father, she nervously scanned the room as if looking for an escape. "Dakota, look at me." When Dakota met Shawn's gaze, her eyes were barren and she seemed lost. "Remember what you just said to me?"

Dakota grimaced. "Yeah, but this will never be okay."

Riann leaned over to them, tapped Dakota on the shoulder, and asked, "What won't be okay?"

"Oh, nothing important," Dakota said quickly, removing her hand from Shawn's.

The moment their connection was severed, Shawn felt adrift. Her vow to keep things simple with Dakota was becoming harder to honor with every conversation. The more she found out about Dakota, the deeper she wanted to dig. She recognized the danger but was too drawn to Dakota's barely hidden pain to heed her own warnings.

The mechanical tiger behind them roared to life and Dakota jerked around in her seat. Shawn caught sight of a small heart-shaped mole just below Dakota's right ear. The scent that had been teasing her all day wafted over her a second later. The hint of musk and spice made her stomach somersault unexpectedly, and she had the crazy urge to touch the tip of her tongue to that compelling mole.

"What is that you have on?" Shawn asked. "It's nice."

Looking surprised, Dakota shifted closer, her shoulder accidentally brushing Shawn's. "Obsession—the new scent. I bought it a few weeks ago but haven't decided if I like it. I was partial to the old one, but decided to try it anyway."

Shawn realized her mistake as soon as Dakota's eyes met hers. Her momentary fascination must have shown in her face, because fireworks exploded in Dakota's dark eyes. An unwanted blaze sparked low in her belly and she couldn't blame it on Dakota. She hadn't followed her "keep it simple" rule and needed to get away. Rising, she said quickly, "Riann, do you mind if I catch up later? I'm still not feeling well and need a little down time."

"Of course," Riann said. "Do you want one of us to go back with you?"

"No, thanks—really, that's not necessary. I'll catch you tonight for dinner."

Shawn scooted out of her seat and hurried away before anyone insisted on escorting her. She pushed the elevator button and leaned against the lobby wall to wait.

A second later, Dakota came around the corner. "Are you all right?"

"Yeah, just tired," Shawn said quietly as Dakota fidgeted with the buttons on her shirt. The nervous habit seemed so unusual for someone with Dakota's normally confident personality, Shawn smiled. "I didn't sleep much last night."

"Me either. Must be the heat." Dakota lightly grasped her arm. "I was worried."

Shawn glanced down at Dakota's hand. The fingers warmed her skin and the air rapidly turned thick. Even though the temperature was mild inside the hotel, Shawn suddenly felt like she was standing inches from the sun.

"Dakota—"

Dakota placed a gentle finger over Shawn's lips. "Look, I know you're tired, but after you rest, could we meet in one of the lounges for a soda or something before we join the group again? I really enjoyed talking to you."

Shawn resisted every urge to kiss the finger resting on her lips. Dakota didn't seem the type to converse much with women who were other than friends, and they weren't. But her offer was hard to resist. Not only was Dakota not coming on to her, she was giving Shawn another opportunity to begin a friendship. Her innocent expression and the memory of the pain that had showed on her face just moments before made saying no very, very hard.

She could do this. Spending time alone with Dakota shouldn't be a big deal. She was a big girl and wasn't doing anything crazy. Besides, they had spent time alone last night and nothing happened then—right? But last night they had *accidentally* run into each other. This request held different implications, different possibilities.

"Shawn?"

"Hmm?" Shawn couldn't think with Dakota so close.

"Nothing." Dakota shoved both hands into her jeans pockets as the elevator doors slid open. "I hope you feel better."

Shawn couldn't believe what she was seeing. Did the confident Dakota Riley actually have an insecure side? She couldn't let Dakota walk away, not when she was sure Dakota rarely revealed this uncertainty to anyone.

"Dakota, wait!" Shawn held the door open. "I'm sure after a nap I'll feel a lot better. A soda sounds wonderful."

"Yeah?" Dakota's face brightened. "When and where? You name it, I'm there."

Shawn laughed, delighted at Dakota's enthusiasm. "How about five in the lounge near the craps tables?"

"Five sounds great. Will you be all right until then?"

Shawn gave Dakota her best smile. "I'll be fine. See you

then. Oh, and Dakota?" Shawn said, peeking around the elevator door.

"Yeah?"

"I enjoyed our talk too."

Shawn allowed the doors to close and leaned her head against the wall. She couldn't be sure if she had made the right decision, but the heavy pounding of her heart and the butterflies in her stomach told her that no matter what, she was looking forward to her not-date with Dakota.

CHAPTER EIGHT

Dakota opted for a nap in her room instead of hanging out at the cabana Terry had booked for the group. At least she tried to rest, but her body had other plans.

She couldn't stop thinking about Shawn. The urge to know if Shawn was okay and if she'd really show at five had her pacing the narrow space in front of her windows. What would it be like to be alone with Shawn? Possibly break away from the group later in the evening? Maybe they could relax in Dakota's room, have an after-dinner drink. If she played her cards right, they might even become intimately acquainted. The thought of Shawn's soft, firm breasts in her hands and a rose-tipped nipple between her teeth made her clit pulse, and she moaned.

Damn all these sexual thoughts. Huh? Since when did she say no to thinking about sex? Shawn was hot. Everything about Shawn turned her on. Damn, this situation was getting crazier by the minute. Sure, she'd love to get Shawn between the sheets, so why would she rather continue their lunch conversation—minus the topic of her father, of course?

Her father.

Dakota hadn't talked about her parents to anyone in years. But then she'd never met anyone whom she felt comfortable enough with to bring up the subject. Shawn was easy to talk to. Too easy. And she'd trusted Dakota enough to tell her about her mom. Maybe that was why Dakota felt safe enough to mention her dad. But conversation instead of sex? She'd truly lost her mind.

Lack of action on this trip had to explain her weird behavior. She hadn't had much luck this weekend in the relief department, and usually when she felt lonely she looked for sex. A hot, warm body always made her forget for a while. Getting off with the stripper didn't count, since she hadn't really been into it—the orgasm had been more a reflex than a relief. Sex and work kept her too busy to remember, and living directly above the restaurant gave her an easy out when memories crowded in. When work wasn't enough, she'd find company, although she never entertained at home and rarely spent all night with anyone. When the sex was over, she went back to her life, back to the no-complications rule.

Even sex wasn't enough to shield her from the pain of her parents' death for very long, though. She still felt responsible. Not being able to save them in that fire—a fire she'd caused—haunted her every waking moment. She should have been more responsible. Maybe if she had been, they'd still be alive. Self-recrimination kept her up most nights, but she deserved that. She couldn't change what had happened, but she could damn well work at being responsible now—at work, at keeping her friends happy, and above all else, at not failing someone she loved again. The easiest way to avoid failing someone was not to let anyone close. So far she'd managed that.

Nothing about the weekend resembled what she'd planned. Even though she felt a little off-kilter since arriving in Vegas, she'd also had moments of peace she'd never thought she'd experience again. She wasn't stupid enough to pretend Shawn hadn't caused them. With Shawn, she felt alive. Recalling their talks, the way Shawn smiled at her, the exciting way her rich laughter seemed to caress her skin caused another warning spasm between her legs. No way could she relax and nap now.

She showered, pulled her hair back into a ponytail, and

threw on a pair of black Lucky jeans and a crisp white button-down shirt. Heading downstairs to the casino level, she was in the mood to test her luck since it appeared to have changed with Shawn. Maybe she needed to try out that luck on one of the tables. She exchanged a hundred-dollar bill for twenty five-dollar chips and waited for the next shooter at a crowded craps table. She placed ten bucks on the pass line and watched the dice roll toward the opposite end of the table.

"Seven!" the stickman yelled over a chorus of cheers. He raked in the dice as two dealers paid out the winners. Dakota took her winnings but kept her initial bet in place. "Nine," he called on the next roll.

Dakota doubled her bet just before the shooter threw a seven, to the entire table's misfortune. The roll cost everyone their money but made Dakota the next shooter.

"Here you go, ma'am," he said, pushing two dice in Dakota's direction. "Good luck."

Dakota was about to fire the dice across the table when someone slipped in beside her and she caught a hint of spring flowers. Cradling the dice, she turned to Shawn and her throat went dry. Shawn looked fabulous in a short strapless sundress that fell to mid-thigh. Strappy gold sandals accentuated her long legs. A single gold chain hung loosely around her neck, the perfect complement to Shawn's wheat-kissed hair. Pink lip gloss dusted her lips, and Dakota needed all her willpower not to lean forward and kiss her. "Planning to try your luck?"

"With you shooting...absolutely." Shawn's tone was playful as she reached past Dakota to place five dollars on the pass line. Her breast brushed against Dakota's arm just as Dakota prepared to shoot, and she nearly launched the dice over the table.

"Damn!" Dakota muttered.

"Seven!"

"Nice throw. Think you can do it again?" Shawn placed another bet next to hers.

"Well, that depends." Dakota shook the dice, winked at

Shawn, and tossed them without looking away from her sparkling eyes. The chorus of cheers signaled a seven again.

"On?" Shawn asked.

"On whether you can afford to lose."

Dakota threw the dice again and this time rolled an eleven. Shawn retrieved her winnings and motioned toward the lounge with a tilt of her head. Dakota gathered her chips and followed Shawn to a small two-person table.

"What would you like? My treat," Dakota said as the waiter approached.

"I don't know. Depends on what you're offering."

Shawn's flirtatious tone caught Dakota by surprise. "No… I…I meant…drink…"

Shawn squeezed Dakota's arm. "Hey, I was just teasing. I'd have to say, though, that color red suits you."

Dakota didn't know what was more embarrassing, her stuttering or Shawn knowing how to bait her. Could this get any worse? She had nowhere to hide from the heat slowly creeping up her neck. She got her answer. Blushing was way worse than stuttering. "So…the drink?"

Shawn ordered a Coke with lemon and Dakota requested the same. Hoping to avoid a repeat of the humiliating start to their conversation, Dakota decided to steer her next question away from her. "Riann tells me you two haven't seen each other in a long time."

"That's right. My dad moved us out to Chicago when I was very young. We didn't see much of the family after that."

"I remember you saying things were kind of rough for your dad—and for you." When Shawn bit the inside of her lip and looked away, Dakota recognized the sign of discomfort. "Hey, you don't have to talk about it if you don't want to."

"Thanks. It was a hard time. Not having family around didn't make things any easier, you know?"

"I can imagine. From what you told me, you seemed pretty close to your mom, though."

"I wouldn't say close. I don't remember her much. I was only five when she died."

Dakota reached for Shawn's hand and held it gently between hers. The sight of Shawn in pain tore at her heart. "Hey, I'm sorry. I wouldn't have asked if I'd known it would upset you."

"No, it's okay. Really. I'd love to talk about my mom. It's just...I have these images in my head and they're all blurry. I want to remember. I just don't."

"I know what you mean."

"Do you?" Shawn sounded surprised.

"I..." Dakota had a hard time breathing around the fist of pain in her throat. She didn't talk about them. She couldn't.

Shawn leaned close, her eyes moist with sympathy. "You don't need to say anything. But if you want, I'm here."

Dakota swallowed hard. She usually ran about now, when things hit too close to real, brought too much up from her inner darkness, but she didn't want to run from Shawn. "My parents died...a few years ago. I only see their faces in dreams. When I wake, it's like shaking an Etch A Sketch. I wish sometimes I wouldn't wake up just so I can keep them close."

"Oh, honey." Shawn twined her fingers through Dakota's. "I'm so sorry."

"Thanks," Dakota said hoarsely. Shawn's touch anchored her as the burning pain in her throat dissipated with each gentle squeeze. Surprisingly, she even felt okay. Maybe a little of the pain had disappeared.

"So," she cleared her throat, "are you back in Seattle for good?"

"Yes. I never really liked Chicago. And you, according to expert sources, have lived in Seattle your whole life. Riann's best friend since you two were little, right?"

Warning bells chimed loudly in Dakota's head. If Riann had been telling Shawn about her, what other aspects of her life had she shared? Dakota also didn't miss the way Shawn turned the conversation back to her. "Yep, ever since preschool. We've always been close. She's a lot to handle sometimes, but I couldn't ask for a better best friend."

Shawn laughed and pointed over Dakota's shoulder. "Speak of the devil."

Dakota looked back and sighed. "Hi, Riann." She couldn't catch a break. All she wanted was a moment alone with Shawn without someone interrupting.

"Hey, you two," Riann said, staring at them curiously. "The girls should be meeting us in a few minutes. What are you chatting about?"

"Nothing," Dakota said, suddenly feeling exposed. Her nerves were raw after discussing her parents, and she wasn't ready for any more revelations about her life.

"Ooh, it's something. You're squirming, Dakota. What is it, Shawn?"

"Just getting to know each other," Shawn said.

"That's interesting," Riann said. "I could help out there. God knows I know everything about this one." She squeezed Dakota's shoulder.

That did it. Dakota wanted out before they both ganged up on her. "I need to use the restroom. Be back in a sec." Dakota raced off, hoping that during her absence they'd find another topic more interesting than her.

❖

"I don't understand. What did we say?" Shawn had a hard time keeping her eyes off Dakota's ass in her tight black jeans as she fled.

Riann smiled knowingly. "Anytime someone wants to talk about *her*, she gets nervous or embarrassed and either changes the subject or scurries off. It's a famous Riley trait, among others."

"Has she always been like this?"

"Oh, yeah. I remember when she was fifteen years old and scared to death about some big secret. I knew she was hiding something from me, and let me tell you, prying something out of Dakota is like swimming through mud. She paled worse than she did a few minutes ago. You've seen that Native American complexion. That's difficult to do. Anyway, when she finally told me I burst out laughing. I couldn't help myself."

"Well, come on, Riann. Spill."

"She told me she was gay!"

Shawn laughed, imagining the young, uncertain Dakota and how different she seemed now. What had created the armor she used to shield that sensitive side? "And?"

"And then I told her I'd known she was gay long before I knew what the word *gay* meant. Shit, everyone knew."

Shawn listened intently, hoping to discover what other parts of her personality Dakota hid away. "Then what?"

Riann shrugged. "Then she asked me if I was okay with it, and I threw a CD case at her head."

Shawn laughed. Poor Dakota. "Was she really that worried about it?"

"Oh, yeah. She always worries about what people think of her. She's just won't let on it bothers her. She has to keep her tough-girl image intact."

"That's good to know."

Dakota appeared beside them and squeezed onto the seat next to Riann. "What's good to know?"

"Nothing," Shawn and Riann said simultaneously.

Shawn couldn't miss Riann's affection for Dakota or the way Dakota obviously relied on her friendship. A little bit of jealousy stirred as she wished Dakota could reach out to her the same way. The reaction was unwarranted—Riann was Dakota's best friend, and she was—well, she wasn't sure what she and Dakota were just yet. Slowly, her respect for Dakota was growing. The more she came to know the person beneath the facade, the less Dakota's bad-girl image put her off.

Shawn's first impression of Dakota had been wrong. Dakota wasn't anything like Alex. Not at all. Dakota's protective nature had driven her a little crazy at first, but Dakota acted that way because she put other people's feelings above her own, not because she wanted to control them. Dakota wasn't selfish or egotistical. She was a true friend, something Shawn never had growing up, but had always wanted. And she was beginning to want that with Dakota.

Dakota looked from Shawn to Riann, her eyes narrowing. "Come on. You had to have been talking about something. What was so funny?"

Riann threw Shawn a look that said to play along. "We were actually talking about the reception."

"Oh." But Dakota sounded skeptical. "Did we forget to cover something?"

"No. Don't worry. I was just about to tell Shawn that the reception is your gift to me."

"Oh, that." Dakota colored.

"Really, Dakota. That's so sweet," Shawn said.

"Yeah…sweet." Dakota looked like she wanted to run again.

"Whoa! Dakota Riley blushing?" Riann teased her. "What's Shawn going to think of you now?"

Yeah, Dakota. What do *I think of you now?*

❖

Dakota motioned for the waiter, needing something stronger than the Coke in front of her. She tried to hide her disappointment when Terry and the rest of the group arrived, wishing they'd all disappear so she could enjoy her time alone with Shawn. But at least Terry and the group could occupy Riann's time and take the heat off her.

"Hey, girls," Terry asked. "Is everyone here?"

"I think so," Riann said, joining the others at the bar. "Let's have drinks and get out of here. I'm starving."

Dakota took the opportunity to scoot over to Shawn's side of the booth when she became tired of shouting over the noise. It seemed like the perfect time to rekindle their earlier conversation.

"So why Chicago?" Dakota asked. "When your family left Seattle?"

"My dad's job, mainly. He didn't like the climate in Seattle, though, so I think it was more that than anything."

Their legs were lightly touching, and everywhere they touched, Dakota burned. "I bet it gets hot there," *kind of like it's getting in here at the moment*, "but is it anything like here?"

"Worse. The humidity's terrible. At least Vegas is dry heat. I guess I'm just a West Coast kind of girl."

"Are you looking forward to tonight? Terry has a lot planned."

"Well, that depends."

"On?"

"On whether we have to go see more men in Speedos," Shawn said, too low for anyone else to hear.

"Then it seems we agree on two things, Ms. Camello, because that's not my idea of a good time either."

They stared into each other's eyes in silent understanding. The look of acceptance in Shawn's eyes meant that they had cleared a major hurdle, and the idea made Dakota giddy inside. Unfortunately, her excitement was short-lived.

"Hello, everybody." Missy hovered behind Dakota with one arm resting along the back of the booth.

Dakota tried to ignore her.

"Dakota," she asked sweetly, stroking Dakota's arm, "how about buying a pretty girl a drink?"

Dakota tried not to flinch at the contact, keeping her attention glued to Shawn. Missy's uninvited caress didn't appear to bother Shawn, but of course Shawn had to have already figured out that she'd rather let a poisonous snake bite her than endure Missy's touch. Dakota wasn't about to fall for the oldest trick in the book. Missy's calculating way might take others in, but she was well schooled in Missy 101. "Sure, where is she?"

Dakota's rude response elicited its desired response. Not only did she jab a thorn under Missy's skin, the look of amusement in Shawn's sparkling blue eyes meant everything once again was perfect with the world.

"Dakota," Riann said, leaning over the booth as Missy disappeared with a huff, "that wasn't very nice."

"She's not nice. So why should I be?"

"Damn it, Dakota, we all have to get along this weekend," Riann said. "Remember, you promised?"

Yeah, she promised. She promised she'd be a good host, not be Missy's whipping post. She nodded, feeling like a heel. Fine. She wouldn't break her word. "Okay, but if she steps out of line again, I'm not sure I can be polite."

Most of the time, Dakota would do anything for Riann, but dealing with Missy was beyond the call of friendship. Missy and Riann had gone through some tough times together in high school, and although Missy seemed to detest everyone else on the planet, she had always been a true friend for Riann, though no one knew why. Riann accepted her as she was and often told Dakota to butt out when it came to their friendship.

Dakota was still dreading the rest of the evening and wasn't looking forward to another male strip club. She just wanted to spend time alone with Shawn without the company of others. Shawn was talking to Terry, who'd joined them on the opposite side of the table, and she looked even more adorable, if possible. Every once in a while, she'd flip a stray lock of hair out of her eyes or laugh, a rich throaty sound that made Dakota's heart skip.

"Dakota, can I see you for a moment?" Riann grabbed Dakota by the arm and yanked her out of the booth.

"Riann, what the hell?" Dakota asked.

"No, Dakota. Do you understand me? No."

"Excuse me?"

"Leave her alone."

Dakota's vision blurred and her head pounded. "Back off, Riann. You have no idea what you're talking about."

"Oh, yes, I do. Shawn's just gone through a terrible breakup with a woman who wasn't very nice to her. I know you wouldn't intentionally hurt her, but she doesn't play your kind of game. Don't mess with her head, please."

"What do you mean mess with her head? What's your fucking issue with me?"

"The current *issue* is Shawn's not your type. Go find someone else. It's Vegas, for Christ sakes! Thousands of other women would like to spend a few hours with you."

Not my type? What the fuck does that mean?

Dakota was seconds from going postal. How could Riann think she would go out of her way to hurt Shawn or, worse, treat her like a piece of meat? "I haven't done *anything*," she said, the words coming out like ground glass. "I'll meet you outside when you're ready to go."

Dakota pushed her way through the crowded casino, mumbling expletives under her breath. She didn't like anyone telling her what to do, not even her best friend. The new reality of her current situation left her ready to hit things. Not only had she promised to keep the peace, but part of that promise included staying away from Shawn. She'd never broken her word. But damn, did she want to.

Chapter Nine

Dakota sat with her feet propped up, looking skyward at the twenty or so performers who hung in harnesses from the five-story roof of the Treasure Island Hotel and Casino. Mystère, a combination of gymnastics, dance, and theater, was guaranteed to heighten the senses and offer everyone hours of enjoyment. The performers were highly skilled, their body control far superior to anything that Dakota had ever witnessed in any sport.

The colorful second-skin costumes were provocative and sensual creations in themselves. The festive music that accompanied the death-defying acts brought a smile to the hundreds of spectators who laughed and cheered at appropriate times. The incredible feats of human strength and flexibility were awe-inspiring. As promised, the show delivered two hours of sheer enjoyment.

Despite the amazing spectacle, Dakota was more interested in watching Shawn, who sat two rows in front of her. Shawn's every move—from the way she shifted nervously in her seat during the spectacular acts to the look of astonishment on her face when the gymnasts contorted their bodies in almost inhuman fashion—riveted her. She enjoyed Shawn's reactions more than the show itself, and oh how she wished she, instead of dozens of unknown performers, was the one putting that smile on Shawn's face. She wished Shawn would study her with such concentration, with such intensity. She craved to be the focus of Shawn's attention.

But that meant she could only be, what…jealous of strangers? That was ridiculous. Talk about a word that wasn't part of her vocabulary. She had no idea what that particular emotion felt like because no woman had ever held that kind of power over her. She just knew that simply looking at Shawn made her stomach flutter and her heart swell more with each breath. The reaction wasn't sexual. Those feelings she recognized. She'd never experienced anything half as intense with another woman. So if it wasn't jealousy, then what?

She spotted Riann turning her way and averted her eyes. Since leaving the bar, she'd managed to avoid her. They'd sat at opposite ends of the table at dinner, her annoyance with Riann only increasing tenfold when Riann made it a point to have Shawn sit next to her. Later, as Riann handed out tickets for the show, she conveniently seated Shawn between herself and Terry, driving Dakota's temper into the red zone. Finally returning Riann's pointed stare, Dakota smiled faintly as Shawn enthusiastically clapped and cheered for the performers taking their final bows. Riann didn't appear amused, but Dakota was past the point of caring. As long as she was keeping her promise, Riann had no room to argue.

Dakota and Riann had never intentionally stayed clear of one another. But Dakota hated confrontation, and if avoidance helped keep the peace, she was all for it. The final applause caused hundreds of stampeding women to run for the nearest restroom. While the group waited in line for their turn, Dakota joined Riann and Terry, who were motioning her over. By the questioning look on Terry's face, this couldn't be good.

"What is with you two?" Terry asked.

"Nothing. Why?" Dakota looked down and tapped the toe of her boot repeatedly into the carpet. Riann said nothing.

"Yeah, right. You haven't said two words to each other since we met for drinks. What gives?"

"Why does something have to be wrong?" Dakota asked. "We were just at a show. How the hell are we going to talk during that?"

"Bullshit! You two are avoiding each other like you're contagious. What gives?"

The more Riann stood by and remained silent, the worse Dakota felt. This was Riann's weekend. Time to pick up the slack—again. "We're not avoiding each other. I'm just feeling overwhelmed. You know these big groups really aren't my style. I'm more of a one-on-one type of person."

Terry snickered. "Yeah, well, we all know *that*. If it's bothering you this much, maybe we should let you off the hook tonight. We're all supposed to go dancing later, but I'm sure you'll find something or *someone* else to occupy your free time. Maybe a beautiful concierge? I may need the ten bucks when this weekend is over."

"No," Riann said. "She needs to stay with us. You promised you'd go along with whatever we decided, Dakota."

Dakota shook her head, angry that her plan had backfired. She'd hoped that by taking the heat for both of them, Riann would feel guilty about her accusations earlier and cut her some slack. "Yeah, I did, didn't I?"

Frustrated and angry, Dakota walked away, needing to regroup. She had to find a way to get Riann to back off and stop acting like Shawn's warden. By night's end, she'd discover a way to get close to Shawn. She had to before she lost what remained of her control.

❖

Shawn leaned against the back wall of the loud smoke-filled room, staring at the soda swirling in her cup. She needed some type of distraction, anything to take her mind off Dakota and the woman she held in her arms.

Dakota had been staying away from her since they'd met

for drinks, and she wondered if the connection they'd made before Missy interrupted them had scared her off. For the first time, she'd seen recognition, friendship—acceptance, in her eyes. The breathtaking sense of union made her want to move closer, to get under Dakota's skin, to know everything about her. She desperately wanted to decipher the secrets that made her such a mass of contradictions. She'd had a glimpse when Dakota mentioned her parents and didn't—couldn't—hide the pain in her eyes. Beneath that tough exterior, Dakota was gentle, even fragile. Of course, she hid that part of herself well. But for a moment, she had allowed her shields to drop and had given Shawn an unguarded view of those deeper layers. Dakota had more to say, which Shawn longed to know, but a bar full of strangers wasn't the best place to pry.

When they'd first met, she'd just wanted Dakota to leave her alone. Now she wished Dakota was in her arms rather than glued to the eye-catching redhead on the crowded dance floor. Everywhere they went she had to watch some other woman in Dakota's arms, and she couldn't pretend it didn't bother her. The first time, watching the lap dancer treat Dakota to more than a dance had turned her on. But there was nothing sexy about tonight. Seeing Dakota and the redhead wrapped around each other just hurt. It didn't make sense, and she knew it. Her hormones were playing tug-of-war with her heart and mind, pushing Dakota away one minute, then desperately wanting to get close to her the next.

She'd contemplated asking Dakota to dance but had been too slow. She should have known ten minutes was plenty of time for Dakota to capture a woman's attention, and she couldn't even blame Dakota this time, only her own indecision. She mentally berated herself for being a coward. Why couldn't she muster up enough courage to walk over to Dakota? Would that really have been leading her on? Okay. So maybe she couldn't act like the woman writhing between Dakota's legs—the body language screamed, "Take me to your room and fuck me"—but she could have managed a dance. One damn dance!

The music slowed, and even though she knew better than to torture herself, she couldn't resist one more look at the dance floor. Dakota and her dance partner had disappeared.

She needed out before the walls closed in on her and she suffocated from the tight ache in her chest. A sea of bodies blocked her path to the front door and panic bubbled into her throat. She couldn't breathe and her legs trembled. She made it as far as the bar and leaned unsteadily against it. She should have been on that dance floor with Dakota. She wanted it to be her, and that realization made her throat burn and her hands shake. Unwanted tears of frustration and fear threatened.

Shawn struggled for air, realizing she'd finally succeeded with her initial plan. She'd managed to keep Dakota at arm's length when she really wanted to find her way into her arms. Thankfully, she was too angry to give in to the tears. Angry that Dakota was the kind of woman she desired, but angrier at herself for not facing her own fears.

❖

Dakota tried to maneuver her dance partner toward the front of the room just to get a glimpse of Shawn. The atmosphere was sexually charged, the fog creating a dream-like ambience for those who wanted to temporarily forget reality and lose themselves in the heady mix of sweat and sex.

The woman in her arms moved sensually to the beat. The signals were all there, and on any other night she would have suggested they call it an early evening and head over to her hotel. But this wasn't an ordinary night, and she didn't want this particular woman. The one she wanted was on the opposite side of the dance floor. Not being able to see Shawn or have her in her arms was driving her slowly insane.

"Something wrong?" the woman asked.

"No, sorry," Dakota said, moving them more toward the edge of the dance floor. Maybe if she could just see Shawn the knot in the center of her chest would lessen.

"You're a great dancer," the woman purred, caressing the back of Dakota's neck.

Dakota attempted to focus on her words but caught sight of Jay and Coal as they swayed in a tight embrace a few feet away. Jay's lips quirked in sexy invitation and Coal's eyes filled with wonder. Their bond appeared so deep Dakota wondered if she'd been wrong. Maybe love like that could belong to her too. For the second time in her life, she felt a loss so profound that her heart literally ached. She wanted—no, needed, the touch of the only person in that room she knew could fill that void.

"Sorry, I've got to go. Thanks for the dance."

"Hey, wait—"

"Sorry, I'm sorry. I can't." Dakota turned and pushed through the crowded room.

She'd made it as far as the bar when she spotted Shawn leaning against it with a pained expression. She should get Shawn's attention and ask her what was wrong like a civilized person, but she wanted out of the fishbowl, away from her friends' scrutiny. She wanted Shawn.

"Come on." Dakota tugged Shawn's hand gently.

"Dakota!" Shawn flung herself into her arms.

"Hey!" Dakota held her tight, too stunned to think, but she wasn't letting go. She sighed, almost scared to breathe—afraid of the moment ending too quickly.

She caressed the length of Shawn's back and slid her hand under Shawn's hair, cupping her neck. "Dance with me."

Shawn didn't say yes but allowed Dakota to lead her onto the floor. Dakota cradled her close, protecting her within the circle of her arms. She tingled all over, and an ache deep inside forced a groan. She'd never been with anyone who made her feel so complete, so alive. They fit flawlessly together, moving not in time to the music but in perfect sync with each other's heartbeats. She pulled away slightly, took in the hungry look in Shawn's deep blue eyes, and tilted her head toward the sweetest lips she'd ever laid eyes on. The music faded to a stop, and the blaring spotlights returned, along with the heavy beat. Shawn jumped and pulled away, shock registering on her face. Dakota stood motionless. Her chest heaved, the thumping between her legs having nothing to do with the heavy bass that rocked the dance floor. She had to say something. Anything.

"Shawn—"

"I can't…I'm sorry." Shawn broke free and bolted for the door.

Dakota's legs didn't want to move. Her whole body shuddered with arousal. She shook off the effects of the dance and forced herself after Shawn. Her pursuit stopped short when Riann blocked her path.

"Dakota, what happened with Shawn? Is she okay?"

She wished she had an answer as she chanced another look at the door. Suddenly, the meaning behind Riann's words sank in. "Why do you think something *happened* to her? We were only dancing, Riann."

"I saw you almost kiss her. Didn't we have this conversation earlier?"

"You know, Riann—"

"Stop! Hear me out." Riann grasped Dakota's arm. "I know the signs. She's got O'Malley blood, and if she's anything like me, when she's angry or hurt, she needs her space. Come on, you know I'm right."

"Yeah, you're right. But I don't care. She shouldn't be alone."

Dakota shoved her way into the congested parking lot and scanned the throng of all-night partygoers, but Shawn wasn't there. She had no idea where to look or even if Shawn wanted to be found, but she had to make sure she was all right and, no matter what, repair whatever had gone so terribly wrong between them. Again.

❖

Shawn sat in her room, staring out over the famous Vegas skyline, transfixed by the twinkling lights and flashing neon signs. Gradually the colors merged into an indistinct backdrop as she replayed her last few moments with Dakota. In those special, private moments she had revealed a mixture of protectiveness and tenderness Shawn was starting to crave. Unable to resist, she'd given in to desire, her restraint had wavered, and pure need had engulfed her.

She'd wanted Dakota, badly. But sex with Dakota would only create a whole new set of problems. Granted, she was supposed to be in Vegas having fun. But did having a good time mean she could make an exception to her "wait until she was in love" rule and have a one-night stand? She wanted to. But this *fling* would be with her cousin's best friend, a person she would almost certainly run into in the future. Dakota lived in Seattle, and whatever happened between them couldn't be left in Vegas. Shawn hadn't come here looking for sex. Hell, she hadn't come here looking for anything. All she wanted was an opportunity to get to know Riann, to spend some time with her so she wouldn't be so lonely.

Lonely? That was probably true. It probably explained why she'd been acting so bizarrely too. After having moved to a strange town, going through a breakup, and cutting off all contact with her dad, she didn't have anyone to make her feel special or loved. Of course, she didn't feel *love* for Dakota. That would be ridiculous. Love, that all-consuming desire for one person and no one else, was reserved for fairy tales, and she was no princess. Obviously, she felt a connection to Dakota because Dakota was lavishing attention on her. So maybe she should let loose a little, do what she came to do, and stop thinking so much about her.

"Okay." She walked to her window to look out at the strip, relieved to be thinking more clearly. She just needed to figure out why was she so afraid to face Dakota in the morning. Resisting her charms would still be a challenge. Dakota was charismatic and so damn sexy, and given her lousy track record with sexy charmers and her vow to make a new start in a new place, being smitten with her was more than just a complication—it was a disaster waiting to happen. Mustering up the courage to start a new life proved she'd changed for the better, right? She could do this. Absolutely. But if that was true, why was she pacing in a hotel room, twenty stories above the rest of the world, angry that she'd completely lost control with a woman she couldn't get out of her head? One she wanted to throw on her back one moment and run far, far away from the next?

The sounds of someone giggling and a key card sliding through the latch saved her from trying to answer. Missy sailed in with two of her friends, Amelia and Stacy, in her wake.

"What a night," Amelia exclaimed, flinging herself backward onto the rollaway bed Shawn had commandeered that sat in the middle of Missy's suite.

"Amelia," Missy said, picking up the room-service menu. "Be a dear and call downstairs for a bottle of champagne. I could use another drink." Missy tossed the menu to Amelia and paused to check her hair in the hallway mirror.

No one acknowledged Shawn, not that she cared, because she wasn't in the mood to deal with anyone at the moment, especially her overbearing new roommate. They'd only met in passing, but from what little she'd witnessed, Missy was one of those superficial people she tried hard to avoid. Since her current situation meant avoidance wasn't possible, she'd try to be tactful when voicing her displeasure.

"Excuse me," Shawn said. Everyone looked at her as if she'd

just transported in from Mars, but she plastered on a smile and kept going. "It's very late and I'd like to get some sleep. If you plan to continue your party, would you mind taking yourselves downstairs?"

Stacy and Amelia turned shocked eyes toward Missy, who glanced at Shawn for the first time.

"Shawn, is it?" Missy asked, her tone one she might use with a dull pet.

"You remembered," Shawn said saccharine-sweetly. "I'm impressed."

Missy's look turned deadly. "Well, *Shawn*. I can see you have a lot of Irish fire. The attitude is cute, but as Riann is well aware, I'm immune to it. So I suggest that if you want to stay in *this* room you follow *our* program."

This scenario was exactly what she'd expected but tried hard to avoid. She was exhausted. The night was catching up to her, and her ability to be civil was slipping like the seconds that ticked by. Normally, she was all for keeping the peace, but the one and only thing she'd learned from her father was never back down from a bully. "Missy, I'm not fond of bullies. Yes, I may have some Irish in me, but the Italian side is more my style, and I don't respond to threats. You are standing," she cleared her throat, "and sitting in my sleeping space. Now, if you don't mind, I'd like to go to bed. Good night, ladies."

Amelia nearly stumbled out of the room, followed by a stunned Stacy. Missy, on the other hand, hadn't budged, staring stone-faced at Shawn.

"Amazing," Missy said.

"I'm sorry?"

"Well, it seems I underestimated you."

"Look—"

"No, really. My apologies for keeping you up."

She hadn't expected an apology but appreciated it just the same. "Thanks. No hard feelings?"

"None at all," Missy said, retreating from the room. "Good night, then."

Shawn didn't exhale fully until Missy shut the door behind her. Missy's apology was a little grudging, but Shawn was happy for the olive branch all the same. This trip was tense enough already without adding anyone else to avoid.

Chapter Ten

Dakota woke abruptly and wiped a shaky hand across her forehead. "Damn."

She kicked off the tangled sheets and scooted back against the wooden headboard, hugging her knees to her chest. The nightmares had returned more powerfully than ever. Her hands shook as she rested them on her knees. She clenched and unclenched them, swearing she could still feel the burns.

The scars were faint but present, the distinct smell of charred flesh permanently imprinted in her psyche. She cringed at the thought of reliving that horror but would gladly accept all the pain again just to have her parents back.

Her dreams were more vivid than usual, starting with Shawn showing up at her restaurant and ending with her parents' death. She tried to remember how Shawn ended up in her dream, how she went from Shawn to waking up screaming her parents' names. She'd thought she was past the dreams and had no idea why they'd returned. Some part of her couldn't move on. She should call Riann, who would find a way to make her feel better. Too bad it had only been a few hours since they'd all gone to bed. With Terry's tightly packed schedule, Riann would need her rest or she'd be short-tempered and impossible.

Dakota jumped out of bed and pulled on jeans and a button-up shirt. She was awake. She might as well be clearheaded. She'd let Riann get her beauty rest—she'd had enough of emotional women on this trip. She grabbed her keys and went in search of an espresso.

Luckily the lobby was deserted at six in the morning and, except for a few flashing lights and some interesting carnival music coming from a nearby slot machine, all was quiet. The twenty-four-hour Starbucks in the hotel lobby was a godsend. If the triple shot of espresso didn't put her in a better mood, she wasn't sure how she'd make it through the rest of the day.

She'd had a terrible time falling asleep after not being able to locate Shawn. A little after three, Riann called her to report Shawn was safe and in her room. Knowing Shawn was okay had allowed her to relax and catch two hours of sleep before the dream woke her.

She finished her last sip of coffee, weighing a few laps in the pool against a hot bath to relax when a hand touched her shoulder. She turned to find Ronnie staring down at her, those hypnotic dark eyes somehow not holding the same allure today.

"I see someone's up early. Mind if I join you?" Ronnie asked.

"Please." Dakota motioned at the chair across from her.

Ronnie crossed one leg over the other, showing off olive skin that seemed to go on forever underneath a classic black skirt. Dakota made it as far as her breasts before berating herself for something she'd done by reflex a thousand times. Normally, cruising a good-looking woman wouldn't have embarrassed her, but for some reason, today it seemed inappropriate. Ronnie, on the other hand, smiled knowingly.

"Are you enjoying your stay?" Ronnie asked.

"Let's just say it's been interesting." Dakota shifted uncomfortably. Her instincts screamed *Beautiful woman! Look!* but her heart wasn't in it. "Do you...uh...normally work this early?"

"No, but I'm filling in for someone today. What about you?

You don't strike me as someone who spends a lot of time alone or enjoys, how shall I say it tactfully, early mornings."

"You're right." Dakota smiled. "But my luck is running a little thin this trip."

Ronnie leaned forward and placed a hand on Dakota's knee to whisper, "Then you might want to stay away from the tables."

Dakota chuckled quietly. "I'll take that under consideration, thanks."

At any other time in Dakota's life, she would have found this conversation ridiculous. An incredibly attractive woman was practically offering herself on a plate, but just like last night with the redhead at the club, she wasn't interested.

Her agitation was reaching critical mass. Was it due to the three shots of caffeine she'd just consumed, her lack of sleep in the last few days, or that she was questioning every instinct she'd lived by since she could remember? When Ronnie rubbed her knee in an effort to get her attention, Dakota nearly jumped out of her skin.

"You seem upset. Can I help?"

Oh, yeah. She could help her, all right. But fuck, she couldn't do it. "I'm fine. Really. But thanks." Dakota stood. "I better get back before my friends send out a search party. Good to see you again."

"You too," Ronnie said, scanning Dakota from top to bottom. "I hope you *enjoy* the rest of your stay."

Dakota heard the note of disappointment in Ronnie's voice and smiled apologetically. "I hope so too."

❖

Shawn lay awake staring at the ceiling. She couldn't get the dance with Dakota out of her head, couldn't forget how good Dakota's arms had felt wrapped around her or how tenderly Dakota's hands had caressed every inch of her back. She remembered Dakota's lips, soft and warm, brushing over her neck. How would they taste? How would she kiss? Would she tease? Would she be gentle, or would Dakota take her hard and fast like a hungry animal after the hunt?

Every minute that ticked by felt like an hour. She was so excited just from thinking about Dakota's kiss that the ache between her legs had become a pounding fist of need demanding relief. She *wanted* relief, ached to let go and satisfy the need that had started the moment she'd witnessed Dakota come in the company of a stranger. That need only intensified after Dakota had taken her in her arms. Just thinking about Dakota's hands as they roamed across her body made her heart race and her clit pulse in time with her now-ragged breathing. She spread her legs beneath the sheets, the coolness of the cotton a welcome sensation against her overheated skin. She parted herself with one hand, using the other to dip two fingers into the silky wetness. Her hands and legs shook as she pushed harder, deeper. Her body began to demand more, to take more. Though no stranger to self-pleasuring, she couldn't get her own smooth fingertips to push her to the precipice. She needed strong hands, demanding hands—Dakota's hands.

"Fuck, why?" She turned her face into her pillow, muffling the sounds she had no power to control. She just needed another stroke, one more to stop the pulsing pressure between her legs that was starting to hurt. Her body hungered and was ready but her heart just wasn't in it. This was getting ridiculous. Why couldn't she simply resist the woman or, better yet, take what Dakota had proposed all along? Vegas wasn't about rules. Vegas was where people left their inhibitions behind and forgot the rules. She groaned. Who was she kidding? Maybe she could have had a Vegas night if she'd taken Dakota up on her not-so-subtle offer the night they'd arrived—before she got to know Dakota. But not now. Dakota was not someone she would easily forget. Never mind she would see her all the time with Riann.

She pushed aside the covers, edgy and aroused. Dakota

would never be a Vegas fling. She just needed to control her libido for another day and one long night—starting in two hours when they were due to gather for breakfast. Great.

She threw on a pair of shorts and a runner's tank top and quietly exited the room. A quick run and a shower would cool her down. When she passed Dakota's door, she wondered if Dakota had returned with company. She couldn't really blame her—she'd run out on her in the middle of a dance with plenty of other interested women around to take her place—the hot redhead who'd been grinding between Dakota's legs, for starters. She jabbed the elevator button, forcing the image from her mind. She'd made her decision. Dakota was a free agent. Who she slept with was none of her concern.

Halfway across the casino she spotted Dakota sitting alone outside an empty bar. She appeared lost in thought until she looked up and caught Shawn staring at her. The cocky look that Shawn had become accustomed to had disappeared. Dakota's smile was tentative as Shawn started toward her and Dakota half stood.

"What are you doing up so early?"

"I couldn't sleep," Shawn whispered, having a hard time not looking into Dakota's questioning eyes.

"Me either." Dakota ran a hand through her hair and stepped closer. Her fingers trailed down Shawn's bare arm. "I've been thinking about you."

Shawn shivered, and the arousal she'd hoped to run off roared back. "Dakota...don't."

"Why not?"

Shawn tried to remember all the reasons this was a bad idea. She took a cautious step backward and scrambled for an excuse. "Because Riann is my cousin and you're her best friend."

"And what does that have to do with anything?"

Shawn had never seen Dakota angry or the least bit unsteady, but she was shaking now. She wanted to stroke the tightness out of her jaw but didn't trust herself not to break her own rules. "There's nothing wrong with a casual thing, but not…" Shawn

caught herself. She'd almost said *not for me and not with you.*
"Just way too complicated, you know?"

"Casual thing…that's what you think I'm about?" When
Shawn didn't answer, Dakota's eyes flashed. "You know what…
shit. Never mind."

Dakota spun away and Shawn grabbed her arm.

"Wait…" Shawn said. "Please, wait."

"Why?" Dakota sounded defeated, the anger gone.

"Can't we just be friends?" *Please say yes, because that's all
I can offer. I don't want you to disappear.* Shawn waited for what
felt like forever but then Dakota gave her a ghost of a smile.

"Well, that depends."

"I'm listening," Shawn whispered, her heart racing crazily.

"Am I allowed to take Riann's cousin to breakfast? Or does
that break any rules?"

Dakota looked uncertain again, and Shawn regretted being
part of the cause. She'd screwed up last night, panicking over a
simple dance. She didn't want to keep making the same mistake.
"No, that doesn't break any rules. I don't think Terry will be
pleased, though."

"She'll get over it." A little of Dakota's old grin returned.
"Say the café in a half an hour?"

"That sounds perfect." Shawn turned and hurried to the
elevator before she could change her mind. Breakfast. It was only
breakfast. She pushed the Up button and pretended not to notice
the way her entire body hummed with excitement.

CHAPTER ELEVEN

Dakota studied Shawn across the breakfast table while she perused the menu. Her ponytail exposed her delicate neckline and Dakota became fixated on the hollow where her neck and collarbone met. She recalled in vivid detail laying her head on Shawn's shoulder and brushing her lips over that smooth skin when they'd danced. Thinking about Shawn's pulse pounding against her cheek and Shawn's hips circling against her crotch ignited a fire that took her breath away. She'd wanted to suck on the soft flesh then, to feel Shawn surrender in her arms, and she still did.

Things should have been different this morning. They should have woken up together in bed and made love, yet here she was having breakfast inside the hotel restaurant because she'd promised Shawn to keep things casual. At least she didn't have to share her with the rest of the group for the moment.

"What can I get you both?" the waitress asked.

Shawn ordered an omelet and Dakota said the first thing that came into her head. "Pancakes."

Dakota pulled her eyes away from Shawn, trying hard to dismiss the urge to become a vampire and suck Shawn dry. The waitress hurried away, leaving Dakota a little uncertain about what to say next. She wasn't used to conversations that weren't a lead-in to sex. This was definitely unexplored territory.

"Pancakes actually sound good," Shawn said, saving Dakota from having to speak first. She leaned forward onto the table and rested on her elbows. "I may have to steal a bite from you."

"You can have as many bites as you want." Dakota sighed inwardly. So much for no sex talk. "What are your plans today?"

"Well, they're not my plans. I promised Riann I'd hang out with her and Terry at the cabana. Don't want to disappoint her."

Damn. She'd forgotten all about the cabana. Oh, well. On the bright side, at least she'd be able to see Shawn in a bathing suit. "If you didn't have to follow Sergeant Terry's orders, what would your plans be today?"

Shawn laughed. "Probably a dip in the pool, followed by a nice long nap."

Dakota suddenly had visions of Shawn stepping dripping wet from the pool, her tan skin glowing in the afternoon sun.

"What are you thinking?" Shawn placed her hand on Dakota's arm.

Dakota gulped, the barely perceptible caress racing like wildfire through her body. Shawn's touch, the way she tucked a stray lock of hair behind her ear, the way she was now biting her lip were extremely endearing and totally sexy. She adjusted herself in her seat, the heaviness between her legs becoming nearly unbearable. "I'm thinking this has been an unusual weekend."

"For me too," Shawn admitted quietly. "I've learned a few things about myself."

"Such as?"

"For one, I forgot how much I missed family. After getting back to Seattle and spending a bunch of time with Riann, I saw how much I lost out on. How much family actually means."

"I understand," Dakota said, filled with sadness. "I miss my family too."

"You don't talk about them much."

"No. But I loved them and miss them every day."

"Then we have something in common." Shawn squeezed

Dakota's arm and let go as the food arrived. "I meant what I said earlier. Friends, okay?"

"Yeah." Dakota smiled. "Friends it is."

After breakfast, they headed back to their rooms to change into something more suitable for the pool. Dakota's anger bubbled close to the surface and she'd had a hard time hiding her frustration from Shawn. The whole bizarre situation left her wanting to break things. Why the hell did she so desperately want a woman who didn't want her? Then again, maybe that was the challenge, what kept her so intrigued. Maybe Shawn was irresistible because she didn't throw herself at her.

But today they'd connected on a whole other level. They'd both experienced the pain of losing their families, and that connection went deeper than flesh. She'd never experienced that with any other woman. Hearing Shawn talk about family made her realize Riann had been right about one thing—she couldn't give Shawn what she needed. She'd already let her family down in the worst possible way. She couldn't live with herself if she disappointed anyone else she cared for. Maybe it was best that they be only friends. Friends meant she would never hurt Shawn too badly, but she still wanted her. The thought made her mood that much darker.

Dakota let herself into her room, stripped off her shirt, and threw it onto the floor. All she'd wanted was a little fun and a lot of action. Was that too much to ask?

She didn't have anything scheduled, and a workout usually helped clear her head. Maybe a few laps at the Grand Pool Complex would improve her mood and, if she was lucky, get Shawn out of her mind. *Lucky? I haven't been lucky since this trip started.*

Since the rest of the hormonally charged party would be spending the day at the cabana again, she grabbed her suit and hurried down to the pool, hoping for a little peace and quiet before they arrived. The Grand Pool Complex was a tropical paradise located directly behind their hotel. Palm trees and beautiful foliage of all types sheltered five unique pools and three large whirlpools. Several small bridges and a waterfall added to the unusually large recreation area, and if it wasn't for the 110-degree heat, Dakota would have spent the remainder of her trip stretched out in one of the padded foldout chairs forgoing the rest of Terry's plans for the weekend.

Each lap drained a bit of the tension away until she'd worn herself out enough to collapse into a lounge chair for a bit of a rest. She drifted with her eyes closed, finally feeling as though things were back in order, if only for the moment. Her shoulders had unknotted and the ball of anxiety in her chest had lessened considerably. Nothing burned off a little sexual frustration like a good swim.

"Dakota!"

A familiar voice yanked her out of a pleasant daydream about Shawn stretched out below her. She cracked a lid at Riann and muttered, "Go away."

"I don't think so," Riann exclaimed. "What the hell are you doing over here when we paid all that money for *those* cabanas way over there? And why didn't you and Shawn come to breakfast with us this morning? I looked for you two everywhere."

Dakota wasn't about to rat Shawn out for spending time with her. If Shawn wanted to tell Riann, fine. Otherwise it wasn't any of Riann's damn business. "All I wanted was a few minutes of peace. Is that too much to ask?"

"Yes, it is. This is my weekend. So stop trying to dodge us and come on. You can do your peace thing with us over there."

Dakota swore under her breath, and the tension she'd just swum off roared back. When she saw Shawn in a light yellow bikini top with a multicolored sarong around her waist stretched out with a copy of *Vogue*, her sexual frustration reappeared too. Shawn was definitely the most attractive woman she'd ever seen. She couldn't think of anything to say with Riann likely to eavesdrop, so she pretended to take a nap, keeping her eyes glued to Shawn as she hid behind her dark sunglasses.

That secret pleasure ended when Missy appeared with three guys and everyone clustered around Shawn's chair. One guy eyed Dakota inquisitively, and she shot him a "not on your life" look. He quickly averted his eyes, focusing on Shawn's breasts instead. Dakota gripped the chair hard. No scenes. Damn her and her promises.

"Dakota, darling, what's with the scowl?" Missy asked sweetly. "Look at this beautiful day and these handsome men. What could possibly have you so upset?"

Shawn lowered her magazine and took a look at Dakota before following Dakota's gaze to the men staring down at her. She quickly dropped the magazine to cover her breasts.

"Oh, wait. I keep forgetting," Missy said. "They're not your type."

Dakota sensed Riann stiffen next to her, probably expecting her to blow up. She was ready to remove the guy's eyeballs with a spoon, but she sucked it up for Riann's sake. Besides, Shawn had handled it.

"Missy, why don't you introduce me to your friends," Dakota said through gritted teeth.

"Gentlemen, Dakota. Dakota, this is Dan, Peter, and Steve. Lucky for us, they're here for the weekend and promised to show all us girls the town later on this afternoon. Didn't you, boys," she said playfully, squeezing one of the guy's cheeks.

Dakota couldn't resist the chance to rain on Missy's party. "Missy, I don't think you'll have time this afternoon to play with your new friends. If you remember, you're hosting appetizers in your suite at six, and it's almost three now."

"What's that about appetizers?" Terry said, arriving with drinks for the group.

"It's nothing." Missy glared at Dakota. "We were just discussing the evening's activities."

"Actually," Dakota said, "Missy was saying she'd rather hang out with these guys than have appetizers in her room."

"That's not what I said. Tell her, Shawn."

Dakota couldn't believe Missy had put Shawn on the spot and shook her head at Shawn. "Missy, you can do whatever you want to do. I'll have the party in my room instead."

Missy shot to her feet, ripping her towel off the chair. "That's a very sweet offer, Dakota, but I'm quite capable of handling my obligations."

"Are you sure? We really wouldn't want to put you out."

"That won't be necessary. I'll expect to see you all in our room at six. Gentlemen." Missy sailed away with Amelia, Stacy, and the men in her wake.

"What was she thinking?" Terry asked, looking at Dakota.

"And now she'll be pissy all night," Riann said grumpily.

"She'll get over it," Dakota said.

Riann pulled her towel off the chair. "I'm going to my room."

Terry jumped up. "Great. Thanks a lot, Dakota. Now I'm going to have to calm her down before tonight. Later, everyone."

The rest of the group soon dispersed, leaving Shawn and Dakota alone. Dakota moved over to the chair closest to Shawn. "Sorry about Missy. I should know better than to bait her, but she drives me crazy."

"Maybe you could resist for the rest of the weekend." Shawn smiled and took Dakota's hand. "Thanks for the rescue, though. She makes me a little nervous and I don't want any problems, especially since she's my roommate."

"She's harmless. Just used to always getting what she wants."

"How about you? You used to getting what you want too?"

Dakota wanted to say "usually" but was concentrating on the sexy curve of Shawn's lips and the soft warm fingers clasping hers. "Not this trip."

"Dakota—"

"No. Don't. I understand. Friends."

"Yeah," Shawn said with a sigh. "I guess I should go help since the party's in our suite. You'll be there, right?"

"Yeah, I promise. See you then." She tried hard to keep the disappointment out of her voice. She did want to be friends. Except, more and more, friendship wasn't all she wanted.

❖

Dakota sat on the couch inside her room, dressed in a wine-colored, long-sleeved shirt and black jeans. She'd added a belt complete with silver belt buckle and her black boots and was ready to go. And stalling. She had to psych herself up to see Shawn and keep her cool. She'd never met a woman who could keep her world constantly spinning, only to bring it to an abrupt halt whenever she wanted. The tightrope she'd been walking since meeting Shawn was swaying dangerously, and she had to find her balance soon. Otherwise, the rope might snap and she might snap along with it.

She wasn't buying the excuse that Shawn wanted to stay away from her because she was Riann's cousin. There had to be more—something she'd done, or said, to spook Shawn. She'd spent a long time studying women. They'd always been her favorite subjects. She was an expert at their likes and dislikes. She'd met quite a few women in the last few days who were obviously interested—the barista at the airport, the woman in the cab line. Ronnie. Then there was the dancer...

And Shawn had witnessed every single flirtation. No wonder she wanted to keep a safe distance.

Dakota bolted out the door. Shawn had seen her flirting, sure, but she didn't see what had changed. That *she'd* changed. She didn't want those women. The old Dakota Riley would have slept with all of them. Hell, she would have handed out numbers and given them time frames, if not invited them all over at the same time. She banged on the door to Missy's suite, straining to hear voices over the loud music playing inside. "Hey! Open up!"

"Dakota, darling." Missy admitted her with a sweep of her hand and a phony smile. "It's about time. We were starting to think you wouldn't show."

Dakota pushed past Missy. "Sorry. Sorry. Where is—"

The air suddenly rushed from her chest and her legs began to shake. Rational thought fled. Shawn stood a few feet away chatting with Riann and was downright dangerous in a short black leather skirt and sheer smoke-black stockings. Her low-cut midnight blue blouse contrasted starkly to her glacial blue eyes. The plunging neckline exposed the creamy inner curves of her breasts. A simple gold chain glistened brightly around her neck. Dakota instantly imagined removing those items, one at a time—slowly and carefully.

Dakota wanted to stake a claim then and there, to snarl at anyone within two feet of Shawn. She wanted to put a big sign on her that said *Taken*. She wasn't supposed to do any of those things, but no way in hell would she let Shawn out of her sight tonight. She didn't care if Riann and Terry dragged them to every male strip show in town.

Riann waltzed over, a glass of bubbly in her hand, and kissed Dakota's cheek. "Where have you been?"

"Huh?" Dakota replied, still in a daze.

Riann followed Dakota's gaze. "She's still off-limits, but doesn't she look great? Dressed her myself, although it was really Missy's idea."

Dakota stared at Shawn. Missy's idea. Of course it was. "Like *that*? Are you crazy?"

"Well, no, just a little tipsy. Besides, we're all dressed like that tonight, except for you, of course, stud. It's kind of the theme for the evening."

Dakota scanned the room. Everyone was decked out in skirts that barely covered anything, skimpy blouses, and way-too-high heels. Everyone looked hot, but she didn't care. All she could see was Shawn, prancing around dressed fit to kill in a town filled with women and men looking for a good time. Just like she had been. Before. Before Shawn.

"What are you drinking?" Riann asked.

"No alcohol for me tonight." Dakota sucked in a breath. Oh, Jesus, Shawn was coming her way.

Riann poked her arm. "Since when did you become a teetotaler? Oh, hey, Shawn."

"Excuse me," Shawn said, never taking her eyes off Dakota. "Terry needs you, Riann."

"Okay. Be back in a sec."

"So what do you think?" Shawn stepped back so Dakota could get a better look. "Missy was strangely nice enough to let me borrow the clothes."

"What do I think?" *I think everyone's lost their mind! That's what I think.*

Shawn frowned. "You don't like?"

"No," Dakota said, "I like. I definitely like."

Shawn smiled. "So—"

The piercing screech of a microphone placed too close to someone's mouth shattered the air.

"Ladies…ladies, attention!" Missy climbed unsteadily onto a chair. "I hope you are all enjoying the festivities so far." A loud chorus of cheers rang out. "Are we ready for some fun?"

"Yeah," the group screamed, waving their boas, drinks, and noisemakers. Terry popped up next to Missy with a life-sized, anatomically correct version of a Chippendales blow-up doll.

"Riann, your date for the evening," Missy announced.

"Riann, if you please." Terry motioned for Riann to sit in the chair and, when she did, positioned the doll as if Riann were giving "him" a blow job.

Everyone cheered.

Dakota blocked out everything around her, keeping her eyes glued to Shawn. She couldn't get her head around the seismic shift in Shawn's behavior. She wasn't against having fun, but

Shawn going out tonight dressed like that? Then there was Riann's comment. She wasn't a prude and normally would have picked up someone dressed like Shawn in a heartbeat. But that was the problem. Shawn wasn't like other women she'd dated. Shawn wasn't a party girl. She didn't do quickies and one-nighters. She was conservative, shy, innocent. She probably believed in forever love and all that stuff. Shawn made her want more than just a fast hook-up too, more than any other woman she'd ever met. She ached to tell her all of this but couldn't. Not with everyone around, and not when Shawn had declared they were on the "just friends" track. She'd just have to stay close to Shawn tonight. Real close.

"Are we ready to go, ladies?" Missy said as cheers of "go, go, go" echoed in the room.

Dakota was the last to leave. She couldn't imagine a worse evening than the one ahead, and she was pretty sure luck was not on her side.

CHAPTER TWELVE

S hawn pushed through the sea of bodies trying to get upstairs to the second floor of the packed club. The Den heaved with people, the same as it had on their first visit. What had changed was Dakota. She no longer scanned the club as if she were in heat. She hung back from the group, quiet and distant. When Riann screamed excitedly from the top of the stairs about lap dances, Shawn wanted to suggest to Dakota they sneak away, but Missy grabbed her arm and dragged her in the opposite direction.

She'd tried to enjoy herself all evening, vowing that she wouldn't allow her attraction to Dakota to get to her. But as Missy stopped at the large stage and motioned for one of the female dancers, she suddenly wished Dakota would appear and save her from the surprise Missy obviously had in store for her.

"Missy, I don't think—"

"Nonsense, Shawn. It's my treat. Have fun," Missy said as a small blonde with enhanced breasts in a skimpy Native American–styled suede halter top and short pleated skirt steered Shawn toward the rear of the room with a firm arm around her waist.

She hated lap dances and only agreed to play along to be a good sport. Just as the dancer guided her into a high-backed chair and straddled her lap, Shawn caught Dakota watching, her eyes narrowed and her stance defensive. Was she angry about the dance, or was that look really one of hurt? Shawn tried to escape but the blonde had her penned in. When Dakota turned and disappeared into the crowd, Shawn pushed the dancer away.

"Sorry, but no thanks."

Shawn struggled through the crowd, searching for Dakota among the mass of people still waiting to get inside. She needed to find her to explain—to correct the misunderstanding, to take away the hurt she'd witnessed or, worse, caused. She ran out the back door of the club where she'd last seen Dakota headed and shadows immediately surrounded her.

"Dakota?"

A hand clamped onto her wrist, and before she could scream, someone dragged her into the nearby alley.

"Remember me, bitch?"

"Who are—"

"Shut up," the man growled, jerking her along the alley wall. The smell of alcohol and cheap cologne nauseated her.

"Please—"

"I said shut up!" He shoved her into the wall and her knees buckled.

"Please," Shawn gasped, struggling for breath.

"You'll remember me after tonight. Danny, Danny, Danny—such a stupid bitch." He pushed against her, his weight suffocating. "Trust me, you'll be sorry you picked that sack of shit over me. I'm going to fuck you so good."

"I'm not who you thi—"

"Shut the fuck up!"

She was only a few hundred feet from the entrance, but the beefy hand covering her mouth muffled her screams. She tried to elbow him in the midsection but he was too big, too strong. Gasping when he lifted her by the throat, she kicked wildly at the empty air. She flailed and lashed out, but he just dragged her deeper into the alley.

He pinned her to the wall with his shoulder and whispered, "Bitch! No one can help you this time."

Shawn sagged, her head spinning. She couldn't breathe—couldn't scream.

He pushed a hand between her legs and yanked her skirt up. Shawn screamed a silent *no* and scratched at his eyes with the last of her strength. He yelled, and the grip on her neck loosened a fraction. Blessed air rushed in and she croaked out a cry. And then he was…gone. Shawn's legs gave way and she collapsed.

❖

Red-hot fury rippled through Dakota as she twisted the guy away from Shawn and unloaded a solid right hook to his jaw. Pain stabbed through her hand but she didn't care. The punch sent him staggering backward but she kept on him, holding him by the shirtfront and landing a hard shot to his midsection and another to his face.

"You motherfucker," she snarled, driving him against the wall and kneeing him hard in the balls. He screamed and dropped like a stone. "Hope I fucking broke them, you piece of slime. I'm gonna fucking kill you."

She kicked him again, wanted to keep on kicking him—for touching Shawn, for daring to even look at her. She wanted to kill him for harming what was hers. Hers. She would have, she would have killed him with a happy heart, but someone was sobbing, calling her. *Shawn.*

"Oh, Jesus, baby." Dakota spun away from the guy and fell to her knees next to Shawn. "Shawn? Shawn, it's me." She wanted to hold her but was afraid to scare her. She carefully brushed a strand of tear-soaked hair away from her face. *Oh, baby. Please, tell me you're okay.* "Shawn?"

"I'm…I'm…"

"It's over…he won't hurt you."

Shawn pushed into Dakota's arms and Dakota sat back against the wall, cradling her against her chest. "You're safe now."

"He was going to…" Shawn curled into Dakota's lap and clung to her as if she never wanted to let go, crying into Dakota's neck.

"Hey, it's okay. I'm here…I'm here."

After a few more minutes when Dakota thought her heart would break listening to Shawn cry, Shawn caught her breath and seemed to gather herself.

"Is he gone?" she asked.

Dakota checked down the alley. Guess she hadn't killed him. Too bad. "Yeah. He won't be bothering you anymore. I promise." *With my life, I promise.*

Shawn clasped Dakota's hand. "You're hurt."

Dakota winced but just rocked Shawn gently. The adrenaline surge seeped away and terror took its place. She shuddered, thinking of what might have happened if she hadn't seen Shawn duck outside and followed her.

"Please, Dakota. Say something."

"I'm fine. Just…worried about you."

"I'm okay. Help me up."

"Sure…anything." Dakota touched the faint bruise beginning to form above Shawn's right eye, wanting desperately to erase it and the last few minutes. She didn't want to upset her, but she had to know. "Did he hurt you?"

"I'm just shaken up." Shawn leaned against Dakota's side, one arm around her waist. She twisted her fingers around Dakota's belt, as if anchoring herself. "Thank you…for being there."

"Oh, baby. Please don't thank me. I wanted to kill him for touching you."

"You made sure nothing worse than a few bruises happened." Shawn kissed the edge of Dakota's jaw. "Thank you isn't enough."

Dakota stiffened. Shawn's lips were so warm, her body so soft nestled against her. She wanted to tell her everything she'd been holding in all night—how much she wanted her, how different she felt around her—like everything suddenly mattered so much more. But she was too afraid. What if she hadn't been there to stop that guy? What if she'd been too late...again? She couldn't survive losing someone else she... Choking on the memories, Dakota buried her face in Shawn's hair.

"Please, Dakota, you're scaring me." Shawn stroked her face. "Say something."

"I saw..."

"Tell me."

"I saw...Oh, Christ! Did that bastard touch you? I saw him with his hand..." Shawn looked away, her expression wounded, and Dakota's control shredded. She jerked back, spinning to search the alley. She'd find the bastard. "He's dead."

"No! He didn't." Shawn grabbed Dakota's arm. "He tried, but you got here in time." She yanked Dakota back to face her. "I'm all right."

"But I saw—"

"Dakota. *Listen* to me. He didn't get that far...because of you." Shawn draped her arms around Dakota's neck and pressed against her. "Are *you* okay?"

"Ah, God." Dakota groaned, kissing Shawn's temple. "Don't you see? I don't want anyone touching you." She sucked in a breath. "No one but me."

"I feel the same way," Shawn whispered.

"Look...We need to talk. I have to tell you—"

"We'll talk at the hotel, okay?" Shawn tugged Dakota toward the brightly lit strip. "Let's just get the hell out of here."

CHAPTER THIRTEEN

They rode in silence back to the hotel and went to change into clothes that didn't feel dirty from the attack. Dakota was already sitting at a table in the coffee shop when Shawn came down, her hair still wet from a quick shower, looking adorable in jeans and a tight pink tank top.

"How are you doing?" Dakota asked when Shawn had settled in with her coffee.

"I'm all right. Just damn lucky you found me."

"I understand the thing people say about seeing red. When I saw you there, with that asshole on you, it was like nothing else existed at that moment but getting you safe and kicking his ass."

"My hero." Shawn grinned wanly.

"No. Not a hero. But glad I was in the right place at the right time."

"Dakota…" Shawn took her hand and slowly caressed each finger from tip to palm. "Come back to my room with me. Right now I want to feel good."

Without a word, Dakota grabbed Shawn's hand and pulled her through the casino to the elevator. She wanted to kiss her right there, but she needed to be sure of what Shawn wanted. When the door opened they swept past a couple who looked at them knowingly. Dakota's hand shook when she tried to get her room door open. Once inside, she hesitated.

"Shawn, we ought to talk about this," she whispered against Shawn's hair, caressing the soft skin of her back beneath the cotton T-shirt. "Shh," Shawn said, placing a finger over Dakota's lips. "Talking's overrated."

Shawn cupped the back of Dakota's neck and silenced her with a slow glide of her lips over Dakota's mouth. Dakota didn't resist. She wanted the kiss, needed it.

She took in Shawn's seductive expression through half-hooded lids. Tilting her head to lure Shawn closer, she toyed with Shawn's lower lip and nipped softly, soothing the bite with a gentle caress of her tongue. Arousal raced along her spine and settled between her legs. The hot Vegas night was no match for the heat engulfing her, and for once, she didn't mind it. Memorizing every luscious curve with her hands, she finally stopped at Shawn's waist, content to focus all her energy on each tender meeting of lips. Giving up control to a woman was uncharted territory for her as she allowed Shawn to set the pace. Shawn needed to call the shots, especially now. She chased Shawn's tongue with her own as it darted between her lips, only to disappear again.

"Shawn," Dakota said thickly. "Are you sure this is what you want?"

"No." Shawn pressed closer, her nipples brushing against Dakota's. "This is only the beginning."

As if sensing Dakota holding back, Shawn kissed her harder, sliding her tongue deeper. Dakota groaned, the urgency in Shawn's kiss stoking her higher. When Shawn pulled away, her breath choppy, Dakota swayed toward her as if the connection couldn't be broken. She wanted more. A lot more.

"Dakota? You're trembling."

"No. No, I'm good, really. You feel so good."

Shawn was beginning to think Dakota was more shaken up than she was. Now that she was safe, all she could see was Dakota in that alley, furious and strong. The memory was quite a turn-on. She'd just had to kiss her.

That kiss. The sweetest, hottest, most amazing kiss.

"What's going on?" Shawn asked gently.

Dakota curled her arm around Shawn's shoulder and pulled her closer. "I can't..."

Shawn rubbed small circles over Dakota's stomach, the touch not intended to excite but relax. The tension in Dakota's abdomen matched the hard set of her jaw. If she hadn't felt the heavy thumping of Dakota's heart against her cheek, she would have sworn she was made of stone. "Can't what?" *Please don't go away from me. Not now. Not when I need you the most.*

"I can't lose you." Dakota buried her face in Shawn's hair.

"I'm not hurt. I'm more worried about you."

"I'm sorry."

"Don't be sorry. Can you talk about it?"

Dakota sighed. "I'm not normally like that."

"Like what?"

"I don't lose my temper. Not that that bastard didn't deserve it." Dakota's voice roughened and she held Shawn tighter. "I just want you to know...that's not me. I'm not...violent."

"And you think I don't know that? I've seen what you're capable of, how tender you are. And tonight with me..." Shawn choked and tears welled at the corners of her eyes.

"Hey, it's over."

"I know." Shawn shifted so Dakota could see her face, see the truth in her eyes. She needed Dakota to understand Dakota was nothing like the man she'd grown up fearing. "I'm not crying about tonight."

"I'm here, if you want to tell me." Dakota took her hand.

"I grew up with a father who drank until he forgot his own name. He was always angry, always volatile."

"Did he hurt you?"

"Physically, no." Shawn swallowed hard. She'd never shared her story with anyone. But part of being friends meant sharing pieces of your life, whether good or bad, and if she truly wanted Dakota as a friend, she'd eventually have to open up about her family. Usually the topic left her numb. But as she clung to the warmth of Dakota's hand, she was aware of every sensation, all of them pleasant.

"I don't talk to my dad because he's a mean drunk. His drinking got worse when my mom died. I look like her but I'm not her, and he always resented that, I guess. I was told she was so full of life, had so many friends. People loved her. I do remember her beautiful blue eyes. When she looked at me, I could see everything she felt. She loved me—unconditionally. I haven't felt that kind of love since. My dad constantly reminded me I was nothing like her, and I just don't want you to think..."

Shawn looked away. Her father had been disappointed in her. The women she'd been with had been attracted to her looks, but had never seen her. Dakota could have any woman she desired. What if one day Dakota regarded her with the same disdain as her father or, worse, saw her as just another conquest? She couldn't bear it.

"Hey. Look into my eyes." Dakota kissed Shawn's knuckles, her expression fierce. "How could you think I'd ever see anyone but the beautiful, strong, brave woman sitting before me now? Hear what I'm telling you. I don't care how your father feels about you. I only know how *I* feel about you. And tonight, when I saw that guy hurting you, I wanted to kill him for touching you. Don't you understand?" Dakota cradled Shawn's jaw, brushing her thumb over Shawn's lips. "*You're* all that matters to me."

Shawn wrapped her arms around Dakota's neck and rested her head on her shoulder. "My protector."

"Me? A protector?"

"Yes, you." Shawn pressed her finger to the center of Dakota's chest. "And don't try to deny it, because I've heard quite a few stories from Riann already. And tonight...with me..." She stumbled on the words. "Tonight, you were wonderful. I don't know how to thank you."

"Baby, I don't need your thanks. I don't want it."

"Baby. You called me that before. I like it."

"I like saying it."

"Why?" Shawn searched the liquid dark eyes. She needed some kind of reassurance, anything to prove that Dakota wouldn't smash her heart to pieces.

"I feel things when I'm around you, things I'm not used to feeling," Dakota said hesitantly. "You *do* things to me—incredible things that no one else has ever done."

Dakota placed Shawn's hand gingerly over her heart, closing her eyes upon contact. Shawn felt the heavy thumping and knew what it had cost Dakota to admit her feelings for someone.

"Don't you think I feel those things too?" *Since I stepped off the plane, you're all I've thought about.*

"I know you feel *something*. I can see it in your eyes when I touch you—when we're close, like this." Dakota grimaced. "But you keep running away. And you said you only wanted us to be frien—"

"Forget what I said," Shawn whispered. "This is what I want."

Shawn kissed her, forgetting why being with Dakota would be dangerous. She was done resisting the powerful force that made her want to crawl into Dakota's skin. She was done denying what she wanted. And what she wanted was Dakota, right here, right now, regardless of what the morning would bring.

"Shawn, what—" Dakota said.

"Shh," Shawn murmured against Dakota's mouth. "Let me do this."

"Anything," Dakota groaned.

Shawn kissed her again and climbed into her lap and straddled Dakota's firm abdomen. Dakota bucked under her, sending powerful waves coursing between her legs. Leaning forward, she bit Dakota's neck, eliciting a groan that made her hotter. She loved making the playgirl weak with need. She soothed the red spot she'd created with her tongue, skimming her fingers inside Dakota's shirt and along her prominent collarbones.

"Shawn…wait," Dakota gasped, pinning Shawn's hand.

"Shh," Shawn whispered again. She trailed a path over

Dakota's chest and brushed her thumb over Dakota's nipple. "I'm done waiting. Let me give you this."

"Give me? Jesus!" Dakota hissed and arched into Shawn's touch. "You don't have to *give* me anything."

"Tell me something." Shawn pinched Dakota's nipple slowly.

"Anything." Dakota moaned, her pupils dilated and darker than Shawn had ever seen them.

"Focus, Dakota." Shawn tweaked Dakota's nipples harder. "I seem to recall you like lap dances. Am I right?"

"Yes."

"So if *I* danced for you, would you stop me?"

"Dance for…"

Dakota's body vibrated as Shawn rotated her hips more firmly into her lap. Shawn switched her attention to Dakota's arms, gliding her fingertips down the inside of Dakota's arms to draw small circles on Dakota's open palms where they rested on the chair arms. Slowly, she caressed Dakota's thighs, stopping to play with the inseam of her jeans. When Shawn swept over the apex between Dakota's thighs, she nearly bucked Shawn off the chair.

"Tell me to stop," Shawn said as she massaged Dakota through the worn material.

"You're killing me."

"Not yet, I'm not." Shawn parted Dakota's lips with her tongue and slipped her hand behind Dakota's neck to remove her turquoise necklace. She placed it on the table next to them and stroked the smooth skin of Dakota's neck, stopping to unfasten the first button of Dakota's shirt. Dakota's swift intake of breath signaled Shawn had her full attention.

"Shawn, I can't take much more."

Two more came undone. "Oh, yes, you can."

"Ah…"

As the shirt fell open, Shawn took her time tracing the tight muscles of Dakota's abdomen and chest as if she were reading Braille. Dakota looked so vulnerable, hands hanging at her sides, chest heaving. Keeping her legs secured to Dakota's hips, Shawn slowly gyrated to the imaginary beat, grinding repeatedly against the coiled body below. Placing her hands on either side of Dakota's shoulders, she whispered, "Lean forward."

Dakota obeyed as Shawn removed the shirt altogether and tossed it behind them.

"Shawn." Dakota groaned, her tone urgent.

"Yes?"

"I thought when you danced for someone…oh, man…that you were the one who was supposed to be undressing?"

"Would you like me to undress myself?"

"No, I wanna do it."

Shawn laughed. "Not tonight."

"Why…" Dakota hissed as Shawn took her nipple into her mouth. When Shawn tugged and bit down, Dakota cried out. "Ah…baby."

"Because tonight you're mine. Shh. Watch me."

Shawn pulled the pink tank swiftly over her head, taking her time to slowly lower the zipper on her jeans. Dakota gasped for air.

"Damn, you're beautiful." Dakota attempted to stroke Shawn's shimmying body but Shawn pushed her hands away.

"Uh, uh, uh. No you don't. No touching either—house rules." Shawn pushed up onto her knees, her navel inches from Dakota's lips, reveling in Dakota's hungry expression. She intertwined her fingers with Dakota's longer ones and toyed with Dakota's lower lip, biting and sucking the swollen flesh. When Dakota's breathing grew ragged Shawn circled her fingers between Dakota's legs in time to her gyrating hips.

"Oh, God." Dakota yanked her mouth from Shawn's. "Shawn…please…I'm gonna come."

"No, you're not."

"I can't…I'm not strong enough for this. Please, let me come."

Dakota shifted until Shawn's leg settled between her own, and rubbed her crotch against Shawn's thigh.

"No, I said." Shawn pushed herself up on both arms, breaking the contact.

"Please!"

"Look at me," Shawn ordered gently, holding Dakota's head firmly between her hands. "I need you to wait, Dakota. Hold on…for me."

"Then let me touch you."

"Keep. Watching."

Shawn inched from side to side, working her jeans and panties slowly down her thighs. Dakota licked her lips, following every movement with wide, stunned eyes. Almost nude, Shawn straddled her and resumed her dance, coating Dakota's stomach with her arousal.

"Take off my bra," Shawn instructed, guiding Dakota's hands behind her back. With one flick, the blue lace fell away. "Now suck my nipples."

Eagerly, Dakota caught the pink flesh between her lips, rolling the hard tips of first one, then the other breast between her teeth.

"Yes, baby." Shawn grabbed the back of Dakota's head, forcing more of her breast into Dakota's mouth. The pressure made her clit ache, and her concentration wavered. God, she was going to need to come soon. "Yes. Like that. Just like that."

"You taste so good." Dakota planted kisses from one side of Shawn's breast to the other. Slowly biting her way down firm flesh, she stopped to admire every curve, every angle.

Shawn rotated her hips faster as a pounding fist of need beat steadily between her legs. Dakota sucked harder on her breasts, and the answering pleasure-pain in her clit shot into her belly.

"Oh, Dakota…I hurt…I need…"

"I know. Tell me what to do." Dakota shuddered. "Tell me what you want. What you need. Tell me, baby."

Shawn moaned. No one had ever given her this type of power. She loved it, but Dakota was holding on by a thread, and so was she. She pressed Dakota's hand between her legs. "Take me—I'm so ready."

Dakota cried out—an animal howl that tore from her throat. Wrapping her hands around Shawn's waist, she picked her up and carefully settled her on the couch.

"Off," Shawn said, fumbling with the buckle on Dakota's belt.

Dakota tore off the rest of her clothes, knelt between Shawn's parted thighs, and entered her in one fluid motion, moving inside her to the rhythm of her tongue on Shawn's clit.

Shawn cried out, scissoring her legs around Dakota's hips. "More." Dakota repeatedly thrust into her and she lifted her hips in offering. "Yes."

"Hold on, baby," Dakota murmured, tracing the sensitive ridge with her tongue until Shawn swelled between her lips.

"So good." Shawn held Dakota's head in place, moaning to encourage Dakota's explorations. A swirling pressure built deep inside, gathering strength with every swipe of Dakota's tongue. When she thought she'd die if she didn't erupt, Dakota released the suction on her clitoris and sent her flying over the edge with a few rapid flicks of her tongue.

"Yes...ohyes!"

Dakota kept her mouth on Shawn, coaxing the last shivers of orgasm from her.

"Come here," Shawn said, pulling Dakota on top of her while sliding a thigh between Dakota's parted legs. Dakota rode her thigh and Shawn gripped her ass, pulling her up and down, faster and faster. Bracing herself above Shawn, Dakota rocked back and forth, a thin sheen of sweat covering her torso.

"Come for me, baby," Shawn gasped. "Let me see you."

"Oh, fuck!" Dakota drove hard, jerking against Shawn's thigh. With a hoarse cry, she collapsed into Shawn's arms feeling breathless—speechless—and a little helpless.

"God, you're sexy," Shawn said, moving a damp lock of hair out of her lover's eyes.

"Sexy? I have no control with you." Dakota panted. "How can that be sexy?"

Shawn tilted Dakota's chin to force Dakota to look at her. "I want you to lose control with me. I want to take you and give myself to you. To me, that's sexy."

"I see." Dakota shifted restlessly, moving to tease one of Shawn's nipples between her lips.

"Oh."

"You are so beautiful," Dakota mumbled with a nipple held firmly between her teeth.

"Don't talk with your mouth full." Shawn hissed when Dakota stopped talking and bit down. "What you're doing...I'll come."

Dakota reached between them, grasping all of Shawn in her palm. This time she worked Shawn slow and smooth. Shawn's second orgasm left her witless and exhausted with just enough strength left to pull Dakota into her arms and close her eyes.

❖

Dakota stared out the window of her hotel room at the glittering Vegas skyline. How could so much change so quickly? She didn't have to look far for an explanation. The woman sleeping before her was the answer to everything. Shawn had changed her. She'd never let a woman take control, never given her body so freely to another. Shawn could take and give all in a single perfect moment. She'd kept Dakota on edge, manipulating her until her control shredded. She'd never experienced that type of high before, never had someone take her to such heights.

Her control was her armor, and without it she felt helpless, vulnerable.

Dawn broke through the dark sky, painting the August morning orange and red. Sitting gently on the edge of the bed, she was content to watch Shawn sleep. Her heart was breaking, but she couldn't mend it. This was supposed to have been an uncomplicated weekend. A few days of fun and a little casual company to pass the time. But this weekend had been anything but simple, and Shawn could never be a casual acquaintance.

Dakota didn't have to understand much about Shawn to know that her willingness to sleep with her meant she'd risked a part of her heart. But Dakota didn't deserve and couldn't accept that gift. She couldn't be responsible for Shawn's happiness. She couldn't be responsible for anyone's happiness. The last time she'd been entrusted with the care of those she loved, she'd failed them. She couldn't trust herself, and Shawn shouldn't trust her either.

"My protector," Shawn had called her. Dakota nearly laughed. She'd almost been too late to stop the drunk from attacking Shawn, and what if she hadn't gotten there in time? What if she'd failed to protect someone she cared for yet again? She'd never survive it. No, it was better this way. Leaving was easier than facing the fact she was falling in love.

Falling in love. She'd never considered the concept. Love wasn't for her. Love was a gamble for people who'd sacrifice everything for a chance at happiness. But she cared for Shawn too much to make that bet. She couldn't bear the thought of ever letting Shawn down—or of opening herself to losing someone else she loved. Shawn made her feel things she'd never experienced before, wonderful things—desire, tenderness, understanding, respect. Shawn made her feel special, but she wouldn't wager either of their hearts on a long shot. She couldn't take the risk.

Slinging her carry-on over her shoulder, she placed a note on the dresser before taking one last long, lingering look at the woman who'd taken a chance on her and laid it all on the line.

Shawn was a lot braver than she was. Silently she slipped out and closed the door, leaving the biggest gamble of her life resting peacefully in Vegas.

CHAPTER FOURTEEN

Shawn hunched over the kitchen sink inside her tiny apartment, scrubbing with gusto as the sponge disintegrated in her hand. She wiped the back of her gloved hand across her forehead, breathing heavily from the tedious manual labor. She'd scoured, polished, and vacuumed every possible spot in the place. Staying occupied helped her forget. The extra shifts she'd taken on after returning from Vegas helped too. Physically she was beat, but she'd take that pain over the sting of waking to Dakota's absence any day. She now understood why people called Vegas the city of bright lights and dead-end dreams.

She threw the gloves into the trash and sprawled across her sofa, closing her eyes to the afternoon sun. The bright rays warmed her skin, but nothing could heat up the cold that had settled around her heart after Dakota walked away. Since returning, she hadn't managed more than four hours' sleep on any given night. When she slept she dreamed, and when she dreamed, Dakota was there just like on their last, and only, night together—attentive and tender and caring. She'd thought of Dakota every moment since she'd returned, and when visions of smoky eyes and knowing hands forced their way through all her barriers again, she crumbled.

She pressed her arm over her face, trying to block the flood of hot tears that threatened. The fist in her throat flexed and she gasped, failing once again to surface from the torrent of emotion that threatened to drown her. Keeping busy helped her forget, but when she was alone, images of Dakota ambushed her.

"Stupid, stupid, stupid," she mumbled, wiping furiously at her eyes. How could she have fallen for the oldest trick in the book? She'd allowed Dakota in, actually thought she cared because she held her, comforted her. That was all a means to an end. And then two words, the only explanation Dakota gave for stomping on her heart. A simple note Shawn had read a thousand times, still not fully understanding its meaning.

I'm sorry. The words echoed relentlessly in her head. Sorry for what? Meeting? Getting to know one another? Sleeping together? Nothing made sense. Dakota had wanted her. She'd felt the desire in Dakota's touch, tasted the hunger on Dakota's lips, eventually succumbed in Dakota's arms. Those few hours were the most magical of her life, and then Dakota had walked away as if they'd meant nothing.

She hadn't seen or talked to Riann since the plane ride home. At first she'd been embarrassed. Being another notch on the famous Riley belt left her feeling foolish and used. Riann couldn't understand why Dakota left without telling anyone good-bye and didn't even answer her phone when Riann tried to call her, but Shawn hadn't wanted to share the details of her night with Dakota. Staying the last day in Vegas, without Dakota there, without someone to lean on, to talk to, had been utterly miserable. And to top things off, Missy seemed to understand what had happened and took every opportunity to bring up Dakota's departure. Shawn was just happy she'd escaped before committing homicide.

She couldn't even really be angry at Dakota for being Dakota. *She* had decided to spend the night with Dakota, even though Dakota had resisted at first. She hadn't expected Dakota's hesitancy or willingness to give up total control. Dakota hadn't been at all as she had expected—she'd been so gentle, so... respectful in a way no woman had ever been with her. But why did she leave? If this was how she treated all her one-night stands, it was a miracle a group of women didn't follow her day and night with lethal intent.

Angry at Dakota and even angrier at herself for allowing things between them to go too far, Shawn threw on a pair of shorts and a white T-shirt. She couldn't take the suffocating loneliness of her apartment any more. Grabbing her keys, she headed to the corner market to pick up food for an early dinner. She'd shop and cook and hopefully forget about Vegas and the fact that she'd gambled with her heart and lost.

❖

Dakota closed her eyes, but the sounds of car horns and people passing on the street below her open window penetrated her awareness. Ordinarily she loved living over the restaurant. She loved the sounds of the city, but tonight the city noises only annoyed her. To add to her irritation, her phone was ringing *again*. Finally the persistent caller decided to leave a message.

"Damn it, Dakota, I know you're there. Pick up the phone," Riann shouted from the answering machine.

Dakota refused to budge from the couch.

"Dakota, pick up!"

"No."

"Come on. Please?"

"Nope."

Dakota hadn't talked to Riann since getting back from Vegas. She wasn't proud of sneaking off because she couldn't face Shawn. She'd gone straight to the airport without saying a word to anyone, especially avoiding Jay and Riann. True, Riann knew her better than anyone else on the planet, but Jay would see her heart was bleeding, profusely.

Finally, home, she succumbed to the emptiness inside. She missed her daily chats with Riann, but she missed Shawn a million times more.

"That's it," Riann said. "I'm coming over there."

The dial tone replaced Riann's voice.

"Fine," Dakota muttered. She'd just pretend she wasn't home and not answer the door, like all the other times. She even refused Jay's phone calls, knowing Riann had probably put her up to calling.

She didn't usually wallow. She'd always been steady, goal-oriented. She'd stuck to a particular path whether in her professional or personal life. Losing sleep over a woman was unheard of, and she never went out of her way to impress women. She'd never needed to until Shawn. She'd finally found someone she'd connected to, and she'd run out on her. Frustrated with her own behavior and besieged by feelings she didn't know what to do with, she escaped to the shower.

As soon as the warm water cascaded down her body, she reached between her legs and shut her eyes. She hadn't wanted to be with anyone since the night she left Shawn, but her body craved release even if only by her own hand. Stroking herself firmly, she braced one arm against the wall, her head hung more in shame than relief. Unfortunately, like all the other times since returning home, her body wouldn't respond. When she finally threw back her head and cried out, it had nothing to do with achieving orgasm.

She cranked off the water, grabbed a towel, and wandered aimlessly back into the bedroom. She probably ought to get dressed, but she didn't need to be at work right away. If it hadn't been for her responsibilities at the restaurant, she wouldn't leave her apartment at all. The sound of a fist striking wood was followed by Riann's "You're in deep shit" voice. "Dakota, I swear to God, if you don't open this door, I'll break it down."

"What part of 'leave me alone' is so hard to understand?" Dakota yanked open the door. She thought twice about verbally thrashing Riann when she took in her ashen appearance. Riann had bags under her eyes and looked like she hadn't slept in weeks. "What?"

"About damn time." Riann pushed her way inside and slumped onto the leather sofa.

"Give me a minute." Dakota went into the bedroom and put on a T-shirt and jeans, not bothering with underwear or shoes. She avoided Riann's gaze when she returned, but she could feel the glare boring into her. "What?"

"Dakota," Riann said, "*please*, look at me."

Dakota couldn't. Not after everything she'd done to Shawn, not after all the messages from Riann saying she'd been selfish and cruel—all of them hurtful—every one of them true. Riann had no way of knowing that not only Shawn's heart had been broken.

"Dakota...honey...enough. I can't take this. You've always talked to me. I miss you."

Dakota kept her gaze glued to the window. She'd been fighting for control ever since she walked out of that room, and the pain in Riann's voice pierced her heart like a thousand tiny arrows. She couldn't handle any more hurt. Not Riann's, not Shawn's, and especially not her own. She buried her face in her hands and did something she'd been doing a lot lately. She cried.

"Dakota, what is it?" Riann wrapped her arm around Dakota's shoulder and pulled her close. "Come on, honey, whatever it is, you can tell me."

"No, I can't, Riann, just...leave me alone."

Riann shook her head, laughing softly against Dakota's hair. "You know me better than that. Since when have I *ever* left you alone? Come on, you haven't said a word to me in over two weeks. Peter says you've been acting weird, you've hardly been at work, and you've been avoiding me like a bad rash. I'm going to ask you again, what's going on?"

"When did you...talk...with Peter?" Dakota wiped a trembling hand across her face.

"Every day. Since you wouldn't talk to me, I had to find someone who knew what you'd been up to."

"Traitor," Dakota said, secretly touched by Riann's

persistence. She swallowed through a scratchy throat. "I need a soda."

Dakota retreated into the kitchen with Riann close behind. Riann sat at the breakfast bar as Dakota pulled a soda out of the fridge and tossed it in her direction.

"So…spill."

"God, you never give up, do you?"

"Do I seriously need to answer that?"

"I told you, Riann, leave it—"

"Yeah, yeah, yeah. How many times do we have to go through this? I told you before, you can't hide anything from me, so don't even try. Besides, whatever it is, you'll feel a hundred percent better if you get it off your chest."

Dakota didn't have the energy to fight. Taking the seat next to Riann, she opened her soda can and took a healthy swig. "I don't know if I can explain this to you. You'll never understand. Hell, I don't get it." *And you'll be even more pissed at me than when I left Vegas unexpectedly.*

"Try me. I'm your best friend. I know more about you than anyone."

"You won't believe me." Dakota held up her hands when Riann shot her a "just tell me already" look. "Okay, okay. What if I told you…that I feel…*different* when I'm with Shawn?"

"What do you mean *different?*"

"See, just what I said. We can't do this." Dakota hopped down off the stool but Riann grabbed her arm before she could escape.

"Stop. Come on…explain. I'm listening."

"She makes me *crazy*. She's so damn stubborn, but she's also fragile in a lot of ways and then she's…I don't know…funny, easy to talk to, and so damn beautiful. See? I'm crazy."

"And is that bad?"

"Of course it's bad." Dakota groaned. "I haven't been able to sleep since I walked out of that hotel room. To make matters worse, I can't even look at another woman. Jesus, Riann! What does that say about someone like me?"

"You tell me."

"God! Why are we friends again?"

"Honey, think about what you're saying."

Dakota slammed the can she'd been drinking from down on the counter. "God damn it. I don't have to think about this. I need her. Don't you get it?"

Riann smiled triumphantly. "Feel better?"

"Some," Dakota admitted. Surprisingly, the heavy ache in her chest *had* disappeared, but nothing else had changed. Riann was her best friend and Shawn's cousin. She shouldn't even be discussing this with her. She shuddered and rubbed her face. "Fuck."

"Does Shawn know how you feel?" Riann asked quietly.

"How could she? I didn't know—not until we couldn't be together, until I couldn't touch her." Dakota clenched her fist. "Now I don't know what to do about it. I left her, remember? She'll never want to see me again." *I destroy the people I love eventually. Don't you get it?*

Riann grabbed Dakota's hand. "Well, I don't know about any of *that*, but you'll never be sure until you ask her."

"Ask her? And how am I supposed to do that? I wouldn't be surprised if she has a voodoo doll with my likeness full of pins in her apartment. Not that I blame her."

"You're a big girl." Riann climbed off her stool and kissed her cheek. "She doesn't work far from here. Figure it out."

"And you won't be mad at me?" Dakota asked.

"Mad at you?" Riann laughed. "Dakota, honey, any woman who has you tied up in knots like this has my seal of approval."

CHAPTER FIFTEEN

The smoke grew thicker, choking her. Her lungs burned and tears ran from her stinging eyes. She jiggled the handle of the door, and this time she made it easily into the large room that she'd seen a hundred times before. This time, though, something was different. Her parents' bed was not in the center of the room and she couldn't hear their screams. Terror clawed at her throat. Shawn stood in a ring of flames, her hand outstretched.

"Shawn! Don't move!" Dakota grabbed for her hand, but her fingers fell short. A loud crack penetrated the darkness. Dakota staggered back and Shawn was gone. "Shawn, no!"

Dakota sprang off the couch, her heart thundering. The dream was too real, the feelings of loss too much like what she had experienced every day since walking away from Shawn. Suddenly, seeing her was the most important thing in her life. She checked the clock on her way to the door. A little past midnight. Maybe time was finally on her side.

❖

Shawn wiped down the bar and glanced at the clock. Already past twelve—the night had been busy and she hadn't had time to think about anything, not even Dakota. That had been a short but welcome relief. The crowds had finally dwindled, and in less than an hour her shift would end. Shawn found comfort with the remaining lonely souls lately, relating to them in ways she never could before. She didn't drink. She never would. But their presence made her feel as if she wasn't the only one in the world suffering.

"What can I get you?" Shawn asked, not looking up at the person who sat down in front of her.

"You."

Shawn stilled. She knew that voice. She ought to—it had haunted her dreams for the last few weeks. She looked up into the unforgettable dark eyes and whispered, "Dakota."

"Hey," Dakota replied shyly, fidgeting on the tall wooden stool.

"Hello."

Shawn turned away. She couldn't look at Dakota without hurt in her eyes. And she did hurt.

"Shawn, please." Dakota lightly grasped her arm across the bar. "I know you're mad, but can we talk?"

Shawn's skin burned at Dakota's touch, and a familiar tingling sensation brought goose bumps out on her flesh. She was tired and her mind wasn't working properly. If she wasn't careful, she would end up in the same place she'd been a few weeks earlier. She couldn't do that to herself again and survive another day. "Talk? Talk about what? I think your note said it all. Don't you?"

Dakota lowered her eyes. "I'm sorry."

"Yeah, that's what the note said." Shawn pulled free of Dakota's grip and walked away.

Dakota followed her toward the other end of the bar. "Shawn, look. I *am* sorry, but it's more than that."

Shawn stopped and glared, gesturing at the few customers still clustered at the bar. "Do you mind?"

Dakota leaned over the bar and lowered her voice to a whisper. "I'm not sorry that we were together. I'm not sorry that

I spent the most amazing night of my life with you. What I *am* sorry about is that I ran out without talking to you about us."

"There is no *us*," Shawn said. "You took care of that the minute you walked out the door. Look, I've got work to do before we close. Good night."

Shawn headed to the storage room adjacent to the bar, hoping Dakota would be gone when she came out. Her confusion was slowly turning to anger and she wanted to throw something, the cases of stacked bottles limiting her choices. She grabbed a case of beer and turned, nearly bumping into Dakota. She recognized that vulnerable, sexy look. Where it had once turned her on, now it only made her madder. "What do you want?"

"There could be an us, if you gave me another chance."

Shawn shook her head. "No, there couldn't be. We're *different*—you and I. It would never work. That night was a mistake—my fault as much as yours. I tried to stay away from you because I knew you would do what you did."

"Look, can we just talk?" Dakota asked. "Please, just for a minute."

Shawn checked the bar—all the regulars had their last drinks. She set down the case of beer, gestured for Dakota to come into the storeroom, and partially closed the door. *Just don't touch me. My control is paper-thin. Don't touch me.* "One minute—I'm working here."

"I missed you," Dakota said.

Shawn's head threatened to explode. "Missed me? That's a shock, since you were the one who left in the first place."

"I know, but—"

"But? But what?" Shawn rubbed her temples. "Look, it was a mistake…us…being together. It never should have happened. It was just a weekend and we had a fling. I knew it then and I accept that now. So let's just move on and forget it."

"No. It wasn't just a weekend. You're not a fling, Shawn, so don't *ever* call yourself that. You matter to me." Dakota grimaced.

"Damn it. Tell me none of it matters—that I don't matter. Tell me that and I'll leave you alone."

Dakota was captivating, standing there with fire in her eyes, waiting to be damned or absolved. She was even more sexy when she wasn't hiding her feelings, and Shawn tingled with the first surge of desire since she'd been with Dakota in Vegas. She wanted to touch her, which was totally crazy. Shawn stepped back. "It doesn't matter what I think. What matters—"

"What matters," Dakota stepped closer, "is that you're the one—the only one—that I want. I'm sorry it took me so long to figure it out, but you're who I've been looking for, Shawn—my whole life."

Shawn couldn't take it in—the room was too hot, they were too close, everything was happening too fast. She had to get away before she tore Dakota's clothes off right there in the storage room. "I can't."

"Can't or won't?" Dakota asked in a softer tone.

"Both." Shawn scooted past her to the door.

"You can deny this if you want, but I know what I want, and that's you."

Shawn spun in the doorway. Like she was going to let those bedroom eyes and charming words fool her all over again. "You know what? I don't think you have anything figured out. And you know something else? I don't care. I'm not going to be a notch on your bedpost *again*. Now, if you'll excuse me, I have work to do."

"Shawn," Dakota called after her, "you can think whatever you want about me, but I'm not giving up on us."

She stopped at the end of the bar, narrowing her eyes as Dakota followed. "And what is that supposed to mean?"

Dakota cupped her cheek and rubbed a thumb over the edge of her jaw. "It means that you're going to be seeing a lot of me from now on, until you finally see what I see."

"And what is that?" Shawn couldn't keep the huskiness out of her voice. Her vision dimmed, and she could focus only on the rich tones in Dakota's deep voice and the path her thumb was traveling.

"That I want you and only you. That you're a woman who deserves someone who will cherish you and be there for you."

"And you expect me to believe that's you?" Shawn wanted to hear her say it even if she wouldn't believe it.

"Yes, I do. I know you don't believe me." Dakota grinned wistfully. "So, starting tonight, I'm going to come around all the time. I'm going to ask you out on a date, every night, until you say yes. So, what will it be, Shawn? Will you honor me with a date?"

Shawn couldn't think with Dakota touching her. She stopped the torturous caress with her own hand, pressing a swift kiss to the palm before retreating farther behind the bar. Hiding her smile, she said softly, "No. Now go away."

Dakota left, and Shawn wondered why her victory felt so hollow.

CHAPTER SIXTEEN

Dakota regretted her decision to join Riann and some of their friends for Terry's birthday dinner about the time they left the restaurant and started up the street in search of the night's entertainment. She'd been hoping to take her mind off the last few weeks and all the times Shawn had turned her down. At first, it was like a challenge, more of a game really. Dakota would ask, Shawn would smile and say no. But after the first week, Dakota no longer wanted to play the game. Now she just needed Shawn to say yes and was starting to question whether she ever would.

The dinner had taken longer than she'd anticipated, but at least Jay was in town and had helped take her mind off things. Now she just wanted to go home and turn in early. At least the nightmares had stopped after she'd confessed to Shawn what a jerk she'd been. Small consolation for the loneliness that ate at her.

"Cuz, are you all right?" Jay asked.

"How many times do I have to tell you I'm fine?" Dakota was putting Jay up while she visited and was starting to regret it. Jay saw too damn much.

"Fine…yeah, whatever," Jay said.

Dakota was saved from responding when Terry ran up and skidded to a halt beside them, Riann close behind.

"Hey. We're not too far from Cowgirls Inc," Terry said,

nearly out of breath. "Let's go have a drink and say hello to Shawn."

Riann looked at Dakota for approval. "What do you think?"

"Sure, sounds like fun." *And then I'll get my chance for Shawn to shoot me down—again. Perfect.*

"Great," Terry said enthusiastically. "I'll tell the girls."

Terry ran back down the block with Jay in tow, leaving Dakota and Riann momentarily alone. Dakota sensed Riann fidgeting as they walked on and answered before Riann even questioned her. "Yes, I'm still asking her."

"And?"

"And she's turned me down every time I've asked her for a date."

"How many times?"

"Twelve."

Riann raised her eyebrows. "Twelve?"

"Yep."

"And?"

Dakota sighed. "And I'm not giving up. Not until she says yes."

Riann hugged her. "Outstanding."

"Yes, she is." Dakota pulled open the door to Cowgirls and held it for Riann and the rest of the group.

They found a table immediately next to the front window. Dakota didn't see Shawn behind the bar. As usual for a Friday night, the place was packed with construction workers looking to unwind with a few drinks and enjoy watching the female bartenders dance on the bar at various times throughout the night.

"I'll buy the first round," Riann yelled over the crowd just as the music started and a twenty-something blonde in cut-off shorts and a yellow cropped shirt showing off defined abdominal muscles hopped up onto the bar.

"Hey, anyone see Shawn?" Terry asked.

Dakota shook her head in disappointment. She most likely

had the night off, which was probably better. This crowd was way too rowdy and bordering on becoming completely out of control. The music had gone from a country song to Queen's "We Will Rock You," and a second girl, a lanky redhead in a short denim skirt, joined the blonde. The noise intensified as men pushed closer to the bar, trying to get within touching distance of the women dancing above them. They started yelling commands, apparently in hopes someone would obey them. Dancers sometimes shed a few items at this particular establishment, and this crowd was clearly looking for souvenirs.

The crowd got even louder and Dakota saw why. Shawn had just hopped onto the bar. Wearing a pair of faded, low-slung blue jeans with holes in too many places and a tank top bordering on illegal, she began rotating her hips to the famous rock beat. Extending her arms above her head and linking her hands, she gyrated as the room erupted in cheers.

"Oh, shit." Dakota shot up out of her seat as if she had rocket boosters for legs.

The group amped up, the guys crowding around the bar yelled louder, and a forest of arms reached up toward the dancers. Reaching soon turned to grabbing, and grabbing meant touching.

"Okay. That's it," Dakota muttered.

"Cuz, you need my help?" Jay asked.

"No, I got this." Dakota pushed through the crowd, finding it difficult to reach the bar. Shawn was probably dancing for tips, but this crowd was getting a little too friendly. No way would she stand by while a bunch of horny men mauled Shawn. Not as long as she was alive.

"Shawn, please come down from there before you get hurt," Dakota shouted as she wedged herself against the bar between the crowd and Shawn.

"I won't get hurt." Shawn raised her arms again, exposing her midriff to the enthusiastic crowd. People pushed and shoved, some pressing tips on the bar, others trying for quick feels. Beer bottles overturned, drinks spilled. Soon the bar was awash with liquor.

"Come on, baby. Please. It's not safe." *And if one article of clothing comes off, I'm carrying you outta here whether you like it or not.*

"Why do you care?" Shawn smiled at the customers, but the look she cast Dakota was cold.

Dakota blinked. How could Shawn still not know? She refused to shout it out in front of these cavemen. "Can we talk somewhere else?"

"Never mind." Shawn shook her head, tears glinting on her lashes. "My mistake."

"Shawn, damn it. I—"

"Forget it." Shawn spun away, her boot sliding into a pool of spilled beer. She lost her balance and, with a sharp cry, tumbled off the bar.

Dakota lunged, flexing her knees and centering herself. Shawn landed against her chest and she closed her arms around her. Relief flooded her. "I've got you."

"Thank you...for catching me." Shawn looped her arms around Dakota's neck.

Dakota pulled her closer, whispering, "I'll always be there to catch you when you fall. I promise, baby."

Shawn pressed her cheek to Dakota's shoulder. "I know how important a promise is to you."

Dakota never wanted to move again. With Shawn in her arms, she finally had everything she'd ever need. Unfortunately, with the crowd gathering around them, the one thing they didn't have was privacy. She eased Shawn to her feet, reluctantly releasing her.

"Can we—"

Shawn shushed Dakota by placing a finger over her lips. She pulled Dakota out of the spotlight, leaving the customers to watch the girls still dancing overhead. "I'm glad you were here to catch me."

Dakota dared for the first time in weeks to dream. "Please go out with me?"

"Yes." Shawn brushed her fingers over Dakota's chest. "How does tomorrow night sound?"

Dakota nuzzled Shawn's neck, reacquainting herself with the familiar scent. "Wonderful, but I don't think I can wait until then. How about tonight after you get off work? I'll pick you up and we'll have a late dinner."

Shawn kissed her. "Perfect."

CHAPTER SEVENTEEN

Dakota must have broken speed limits to get home, change, and make it back to Shawn's just after eleven. When the knock sounded on her door, Shawn was just getting out of the shower. She threw on a robe and realized too late the water she hadn't toweled off was making it cling in embarrassing places. "Hi," she said shyly, holding the door open for Dakota.

"Hi," Dakota said, her voice husky as her gaze dropped for an instant. She jerked her eyes up. "I'm early, I guess."

"I'm sorry. I didn't hear the door. I was in the shower."

"I can see that," Dakota murmured.

Shawn's nipples hardened. Dakota looked like a starving person in need of a sandwich. "I should...ah...go get changed. Come on in, I won't be long."

"Don't worry, I'll wait." Dakota settled on the sofa and crossed her legs at the ankle.

Shawn didn't move, flushing as Dakota took in every inch of her. If her nipples got any harder they'd poke right through her robe. "I better go."

"Maybe you should," Dakota said in a hungry voice that made Shawn's toes curl.

Shawn fled to the bathroom and slammed the door behind her. She rested unsteadily against it, trying to calm her racing heart. Dakota was magnificent. Dressed in black jeans, a black

T-shirt, and scuffed black boots, she was the picture of the cool, calm, and deadly huntress once again, eyeing her prey. This time, though, the prey wanted to be captured.

You can do this, Shawn. You can do this. It's just a late dinner. What could possibly happen? Shawn stared at her reflection in the mirror. *Exactly what you want to happen, and that's what's scaring you to death.*

❖

Dakota made sure Shawn was secure in her seat before pulling her black pickup away from the curb. Shawn sat silently, staring out the window.

"You look breathtaking," Dakota said thickly, savoring the way Shawn's silk dress clung to her breasts.

"Stop." Shawn kept her eyes glued to everything and anything out the window.

"Why?" Dakota took one of Shawn's hands.

"Because if you don't stop looking at me like that, or stop making comments about how beautiful I am, or stop *touching* me"—Shawn gasped when Dakota traced a finger on the inside of her palm—"like that, I'm going to jump you right here, which would surely cause an accident."

"I can always get another car," Dakota teased as Shawn shuddered under her touch. She continued the lingering caress, running a fingertip slowly up and down Shawn's arm. She couldn't stop touching her. She had gone without the simple pleasure for too long.

"Dakota, I'm not kidding."

"Hold that thought." Dakota turned into the familiar parking lot, taking the first stall and cutting the power to the engine. Silence replaced the roar of pure power. Dakota turned to face Shawn. "We're here."

Shawn looked up at the sign. "We're eating here? The lights are out."

"Yes, we are." Dakota jumped out, hurried around, and opened Shawn's door. "Come on."

Shawn took her extended hand and Dakota led her toward the front entrance, holding the door open for her. A perplexed look washed over Shawn's face as she glanced around the empty restaurant, dark except for the glow of a single candle.

"Where is everyone?"

"No one will be here tonight except us." Dakota settled Shawn's arm into the crook of her elbow and led her to their table. "This dinner is about us."

"Oh, Dakota," Shawn said, her hoarse voice catching.

"I wanted to show you how much you mean to me. I hope you don't mind." Dakota turned Shawn to face her, the glow of the candle decorating the room in shadows. "Do you know how incredibly amazing you are? I can't believe you're here with me tonight." Dakota caressed Shawn's bare arms. "It's almost like a dream."

"For me too."

Dakota placed a kiss next to the simple drop diamond necklace that hung delicately around Shawn's neck. She was about to travel upward when the door to the kitchen creaked open and a waiter emerged wearing a black tuxedo with a white cloth draped over his left arm. Shawn stifled a laugh at Dakota's frustrated expression.

"Please, sit," Dakota said, sliding into the booth next to Shawn.

"Shall I?" Peter asked, motioning to Dakota as to whether he should open the bottle of sparkling apple cider.

Dakota looked over at Shawn for her confirmation, seeing by the twinkle in her eye she appreciated Dakota thinking about her no-drinking rule. "Yes, thank you. Peter, I'd like you to meet my date. Shawn Camello, this is Peter Montori, my right-hand man and maitre d' here at the restaurant."

Shawn held out her hand. "Pleased to meet you, Peter."

"It is very nice to meet you, Ms. Camello." Peter shook the

outstretched hand. "Now if you'd excuse me, dinner will be ready momentarily."

"Is everything all right?" Dakota asked after Peter left. Shawn's eyes sparkled like two perfect sapphires. Dakota ached to run her fingers through the wisps of hair that framed her face, but she held back, fearing that one touch wouldn't be enough.

"Everything is amazing," Shawn murmured.

The soup arrived, followed shortly by the main course of Hawaiian escolar in a rich butter sauce. Dakota watched in pleasure as Shawn sampled the house specialty.

"Oh, this is wonderful."

"Thank you." Dakota grinned. "You might want to thank our chef, Eddie, because he's the one who made it."

"Maybe I will later." Shawn rested her palm possessively on top of Dakota's thigh. Dakota trembled under her fingers, and Shawn liked that. So far Dakota had been taking all the chances. Now it was time to show her she wasn't alone in her feelings. "But right now, I'd like to thank you."

Shawn kept the kiss unhurried, gently exploring Dakota's soft, warm mouth. When the kiss turned hungry, she let it, stroking the length of Dakota's thigh.

Dakota pulled away, her chest heaving. "Shawn...we should...oh, man...finish dinner."

Shawn backed away, stroking the worry lines from Dakota's face. Had she caused the mixture of pleasure and pain she saw? "Dakota, what is it?"

"You just don't know the power you have over me. It's a little overwhelming sometimes."

"Is that bad?"

"No. Yes. I..."

Shawn heard the tentativeness in Dakota's voice. "I'm sorry. I thought—"

"No, I'm not saying this right. Nothing's wrong. In fact, everything's perfect. You're perfect. I just wanted to give you this night as a gift."

"Tonight *is* perfect. Can't you tell? I love that you thought of doing this for me. It's just…"

What?"

Shawn slid closer. She couldn't bear to be anywhere but near her now. "I want to get to know everything about you, even the things that make you uncomfortable, and I can tell you're holding back."

Dakota trapped Shawn's hand between her own, holding it firmly in her lap. "Really? You really want to know?"

"Really."

Dakota took a deep breath, ready to tell Shawn anything. She wanted to give Shawn the key to her heart, to open up any part of her life that Shawn desired. She just hoped that after years of guarding her secrets, she could give Shawn what she was asking for. "What would you like to know?"

"Well, for starters, tell me about your family."

Dakota instinctively withdrew. "Riann is my family."

"Hey, it's okay," Shawn said softly, squeezing Dakota's hand. "I'm sorry."

"No…it's not okay. I want to tell you. I do. It's just…I'm not used to talking about this with anyone, not even Riann."

"I'm here for you. If you want me to be."

Dakota clung to Shawn's hand, trying not to crush her smaller fingers. "My family…died…in an accident." Dakota braced for the pain that usually followed, but the agony wasn't as incapacitating as usual. Maybe Shawn's hand, holding on to her, anchored her against the heavy tide of emotions.

"Oh, Dakota. I'm so sorry. Tell me."

"I will. I promise. But not tonight. I want tonight to be just about us, okay?"

"Anything you want," Shawn said huskily, kissing Dakota again. The kiss was tentative at first, but quickly became insistent with each stroke of her tongue.

"Shawn," Dakota whispered, her body humming.

"Yes."

Dakota claimed Shawn's mouth hungrily, pulling Shawn as close to her as the booth would allow. She took Shawn's lower lip between her teeth, tugging gently on the swollen flesh. Shawn broke the kiss, nipping her way along Dakota's jaw, exchanging teeth for lips as she made her way along the ridges of Dakota's ear. Dakota moaned helplessly but somehow found the strength to pull away. "Baby, we gotta stop."

"Why?" Shawn traveled her way down Dakota's neck, scoring her with her teeth. Dakota shuddered, and Shawn cradled her face with both hands. "Why?"

Dakota's vision was hazy. "Because I want you. So much. But we should slow down. At least finish dinner." She smiled to take any sting from her statement.

"Are you sure?" Shawn nipped at Dakota's lower lip again, sliding her tongue over the soft bite. "Really sure?"

"Hell, no. I'm not sure. But the next time we make love, I want us both to be ready."

"What exactly do you think I'm not ready for?" Shawn pulled away, her confusion evident. "You spend weeks courting me, making me believe we could have something special—that you're the one I've been waiting for my whole life. Then I give you that chance and you're pushing me away? Again?"

"Oh, baby, no. Is that what you think?" Dakota wrapped an arm around Shawn's shoulders, pulling her into her arms. Distance between them now would kill her. "I'm not pushing you away. I just want to take things slow. I want you to know we're together for more than a night."

"Really?"

"Yes, really."

Shawn relaxed perceptibly, settling her head on Dakota's shoulder. "I'm not sure how I feel about this new, mature Dakota."

Dakota laughed. "Not all that mature. I'm going to spend a lot of time…thinking…about you."

"Good." Shawn kissed Dakota. "Now feed me some of this wonderful food."

"Anything you want." Dakota reached for a fork, arousal beating through her. She couldn't believe she'd just turned Shawn down. She wanted Shawn with everything in her, but she needed to be sure Shawn believed that too. She never wanted Shawn to think of herself as a conquest or believe that what happened between them was just sex. Shawn was worth waiting for.

❖

Shawn dropped onto the couch, her insides on fire. She considered putting the flames out herself but knew it would never be enough. The woman she'd just had dinner with was not the playgirl who'd sauntered into the Vegas airport, turning every woman's head and loving it.

But the next time we make love, I want us both to be ready. Shawn smiled. Dakota was trying to prove that she had changed, and she had. The playgirl would have never left a willing woman on her doorstep. "Oh, baby," Shawn whispered. "You *are* ready, and so am I."

CHAPTER EIGHTEEN

Saturday night was always the busiest night of the week at Santini's, and Dakota was happy she had used all her repressed sexual energy to get the restaurant and bar stocked before opening at five. Peter was running around like a maniac, and if he had had hair, he would have pulled it out.

"Peter, relax. We've been busy before," Dakota said, giving him a friendly pat on his shoulder.

"Oh, sure, coming from the person who barely works here anymore. By the way, why *are* you here?"

Dakota wondered the same thing. She couldn't believe she had been able to walk away the night before, leaving Shawn breathless on her doorstep. The thought of what she'd really wanted to do had kept her awake all night, so she hadn't stopped, hoping that eventually she'd be too tired to think. So far that hadn't worked. "Well, I planned to go take a nap, but then I saw how busy we are, so I decided to stay."

"Ha! Nice try. I may be busy, but I'm not blind. After last night, this was the last place I expected you to be."

Me too. "Yeah, well, get back to work. Table three needs water," Dakota said sweetly, pointing her chin in the direction of the dining area.

"Oh, yes, ma'am," he answered mockingly, flinging his dish towel over his shoulder as he sauntered back into the dining room.

Dakota chuckled softly, thanking whatever deity was

listening that she had the type of friends she did. She walked behind the bar to pile up the cleaned stacks of glasses where the bartender could get to them. She was busy rotating the stock when she heard a soft voice.

"Excuse me?"

Dakota's head was below the counter, but she didn't need to look up to recognize that sweet sound. She knew all about that voice and the power it had to touch her like a caress. It was the same voice she was slowly coming to love.

Dakota shot up, catching the metal end of one of the glass strainers with her forehead. "Ouch!"

"Honey?" Shawn hurried around the bar. "Are you all right?"

"Yeah." Dakota knelt with one hand covering her eye, not feeling a bit of pain. *Honey. She called me honey.* "That was graceful."

"Here, let me see." Shawn eased Dakota's hand away from her face. "You've got a small cut above your right eye. I don't think it needs stitches."

Dakota forgot all about her forehead the minute Shawn touched her. The steady pulse of arousal that had started at the beginning of their date last night was now a full beat away from making her embarrassing moment even more humiliating. Her thighs shook so badly that if she were standing, she would have toppled over.

"Hey," Dakota said darkly, her gaze unfocused.

"Hey, yourself."

"We need to go somewhere else." Dakota rose unsteadily, offering Shawn a hand up. "I need to kiss you."

"How's your head?" Shawn asked, her eyes a little glazed.

Dakota grabbed Shawn's hand and tugged her out from behind the bar. "My *head* is fine. Come on, my apartment is upstairs."

Dakota led Shawn up the back stairs to her place, holding her hand, afraid she might disappear. The instant she closed the door,

Shawn pinned her against it. "What happened to you wanting us to be ready?"

"I'm an idiot."

Shawn laughed. "I'm not arguing."

"Can you forget what I—"

Shawn shut her up with a fiery kiss that ignited a chain reaction along every nerve in her body. She spun Shawn around so she was the one pinned, pressing her leg between Shawn's.

"Oh." Shawn buried her hands in Dakota's hair, holding on as she pushed down hard onto Dakota's thigh. "Oh, I'm so close already."

"Wait, baby, wait." Dakota stilled the motion of Shawn's hips with shaky hands.

"I'm tired of waiting." Shawn sucked Dakota's lower lip into her mouth and bit the already swollen tissue. She stole one more kiss before pushing Dakota slightly away.

"Damn, you make me crazy." Dakota ran her hands down Shawn's sides to her hips.

"Ditto."

Dakota shuddered at the feel of Shawn's tense nipples against her chest. "I want you so much."

"Then what is it?" Shawn asked. "You're shaking, baby."

"I want you."

"But?"

"No *buts*. I just don't want to hurt you." Dakota's throat threatened to close but she had to say it. "I don't want to let you down. It's who I am. I let down everyone I love."

Shawn hugged Dakota tighter. "You won't."

"How do you know that?"

"It's simple. Because you promised."

Dakota wanted it to be that simple. She wanted Shawn to trust her, but she didn't trust herself. "If you knew me, you might not want to take a chance on me."

"Then I guess you'll have to take a chance too," Shawn whispered, "and tell me what you're afraid of."

Chapter Nineteen

Dakota clung to Shawn's hand and pulled her over to the sofa. Seated with Shawn close to her, she cradled Shawn's hand in her lap. She didn't look at Shawn, she couldn't. The time had finally come to share her secret, but she feared Shawn would never look at her the same way again. Hell, she could barely look at herself in a mirror and not wonder why she had survived and they didn't.

Dakota's vision dimmed, as if a cloud had passed, casting dark shadows over her. Her jaw trembled and she ran her hand through her hair, searching for balance.

"Hey, it's okay, sweetie. I'm here."

Tears as hot as fire ran down Dakota's face. She didn't bother to wipe them away. She knew they wouldn't stop. "My parents died in a fire I started. I left the stove on downstairs. They were sleeping and I tried, I *tried*, but I couldn't save them. I *killed...*"

Dakota doubled over, the familiar pain knifing through her. She cried for the years of pain she'd carried alone, for the ones she'd lost and the ones she feared she'd lose if they knew. Riann, Jay—Shawn. But this time, she wasn't alone. Shawn rocked her, held her tight within the circle of her arms, her tears dampening Dakota's hair.

"You tried, baby. They loved you and they know you tried."

"They trusted me," Dakota choked out.

"Of course they did. Love and trust, honey. They go together."

Dakota straightened, pulling out of Shawn's arms. How could Shawn ever love her or trust her after knowing what she had done? "Thanks for listening. We probably should call it a night. I'll take you down."

She made it two steps from the sofa before Shawn grabbed her and roughly spun her around. "Just where are you going?"

"I thought—" Dakota had never seen Shawn look so angry. It was scary but sexy as hell.

"You thought...what? That I would walk away from you because of a terrible accident? That you should take the blame for something that wasn't your fault? What kind of person do you think I am, Dakota? Do you really think so little of me?"

Dakota couldn't comprehend Shawn's reasoning. "Shawn, it *was* my fault. Don't you see? They would still be alive if it wasn't for me."

"Dakota, you don't know that."

"Yes, I do!" Dakota paced the room. "The fire department said a gas leak from the stove ignited something in the kitchen. *I* was the last one up that night and I don't remember turning off the stove. I tried to get to them. Oh, God...I tried."

"I know," Shawn whispered, wrapping her arms around her. "Anything could have caused that fire. Your parents loved you, and no matter the cause, I know you didn't hurt them intentionally." Shawn turned over Dakota's hands, tracing the faint scarring with her fingers. "You tried to protect them just like you try to protect everyone you love. It was an accident, sweetie. You have to believe that."

Dakota took a shuddering breath, feeling exposed and embarrassed. She was glad she'd told Shawn everything, but that didn't lessen her anxiety. "I'm sorry. I didn't mean for that to happen...to be like that...in front of you. I'm sorry."

Shawn brushed a strand of hair from Dakota's forehead. "There's no need. I like being here for you, like this. You let me see a part of you that I know you've never shared with anyone. You've allowed me to see you, in here." She pressed her hand over Dakota's heart. "Thank you, for trusting me enough to share that with me."

"Oh, Shawn," Dakota said wearily. "Don't you see? What if I hurt you too?"

Shawn placed her forehead against Dakota's, holding her face firmly in her hands. "Is that why you stayed away from me…walked out on me in Vegas?"

Dakota closed her eyes and nodded.

"Dakota, look at me."

When she did, she thought her heart would stop. Shawn's gaze was strong and sure, and Dakota knew Shawn saw the real her. "I was certain you wouldn't want me if you knew."

"I don't want to stop this and neither do you. If you did, you wouldn't have come looking for me in the first place. I know you left because you thought you were protecting me. Because that's what you do. But what you don't get is that I love you. Nothing on this earth will *ever* stop me from loving you. I trust you with my heart and my life."

"Why?" Dakota swallowed hard, her heart thudding heavily. Her vision dimmed, and a new pounding, a more pleasurable beat, stirred between her legs. "Did you just say you loved me?"

Shawn didn't answer. Instead, she pushed Dakota backward onto the couch, falling expertly between her parted thighs. When Shawn kissed her, Dakota surrendered, knowing that even if she wanted to, she couldn't go back. The last of her restraint sifted like sand through Shawn's talented fingers. "Shawn, please, you're killing me. I can't…Shawn, you gotta stop. I can't keep doing this with you."

"Doing what?" Shawn nipped at the supple skin of Dakota's neck.

"This. Because *I* can't stop anymore." Dakota kept her hands glued to Shawn's waist. Her intention to let Shawn take the lead had been good at first, but this was too much. She had just bared her soul and now she needed Shawn's touch to heal everything in her that once hurt.

"Who asked you to stop?" Shawn said, pushing Dakota farther into the cushions before jumping up. She started to unbutton her shirt.

"Shawn," Dakota warned her, her gaze glued to the tight tank. "What are you doing?"

"I told you before, I'm tired of waiting." Shawn parted her shirt. "If you want this, Dakota, come and get it."

Chapter Twenty

Shawn backed up in the direction of Dakota's bedroom, watching the change come over her. She looked fierce, wild. This was the person she had wanted since that day at the airport. This was the huntress, dangerous and sexy as hell. Shawn's heart leapt when Dakota nearly vaulted from the couch and caught her at the bedroom door. Dakota pinned her against the frame with her lean body, one leg between Shawn's parted thighs.

"I want—"

"No," Dakota growled. "I *want* this time. Don't move." She licked her way down Shawn's neck. She nipped at the soft skin along Shawn's collarbone, forcing her bra up to expose her breasts.

"Dakota, let me take this off," Shawn moaned.

"No." Dakota grabbed Shawn's hands and held them securely over her head. "I want you. My way. My rules."

"Yes, God, yes."

Dakota took her time exploring Shawn's breasts, alternating between biting and licking until Shawn's nipples were tight, hard knots. Shawn's breathing hitched, her breasts straining against the constricting material.

"Dakota, please. I need this off."

"Don't move."

Shawn squirmed helplessly as Dakota removed her bra,

throwing it behind them. She thrust against Dakota, her body
reacting in ways she never knew possible. She wanted Dakota
to take her, wanted Dakota to make her come. She was wet and
she was hard and Dakota's leg between hers was almost enough
to push her over. Almost. She writhed, the steady pressure so
good.

"Ah, ah, ah, not until I say." Dakota pulled back and
skimmed her free hand down past Shawn's navel. She tugged on
the waistband of Shawn's jeans, popping open the first button.

"Dakota," Shawn whispered as her clit jumped in
expectation.

Dakota spun her around so her stomach was against the cold
wall, pressing against her nipples and making them even harder.

"Ah, baby, please."

"Tell me what you want." Dakota's hand traveled lower. She
reached past all Shawn's barriers and slid two fingers on either
side of Shawn's clitoris, gently stroking her swollen lips. When
she grabbed Shawn between her thumb and finger, she wrapped
one arm around her middle to hold her up.

"Dakota, I need you…inside."

Shawn's body throbbed. Her legs weakened. Her heart raced
out of control. Every glide of Dakota's fingers against her pulsing
flesh made her arch backward, trying to meet the demands of
Dakota's insistent strokes. With her arms still pinned, she
relinquished control. For the first time in her life she wanted to be
the huntress's trophy, to be stalked, claimed, eaten alive, inside
and out.

"That's it, baby." Shawn panted. "That feels so good."

Dakota ground against Shawn, the movement adding extra
pressure between Shawn's legs. Suddenly, Dakota's thrusts
became unrelenting, urgent. Dakota's breath was hot in her
ear, her moans alerting Shawn to her plight. She spun around,
walking Dakota backward until they both collapsed onto the bed.
She quickly shed her jeans as Dakota sucked her nipples. "Oh,"
Shawn cried as Dakota pushed into her. "Deeper."

"How deep?"

"So deep your fingers touch my soul."

"Oh, fuck, yes!" Dakota added another finger and Shawn covered Dakota's hand, the added pressure forcing her to crest. But she needed more.

"Put your mouth on me."

Dakota moved between Shawn's legs, taking her with abandon. Shawn braced as the orgasm swirled within, tensing as she peaked. Spasm after spasm coursed through her quaking body. She held Dakota's head in place, every swipe of Dakota's tongue making her even more helpless. She whimpered as Dakota sucked at her sweet spot, milking her of every last tremor. "Baby, you gotta stop."

"Why?" Dakota kissed her way back up Shawn's body and pulled her into her arms with a contented sigh. "You taste so sweet."

Gasping for breath, Shawn willed her limbs to move, but they wouldn't obey her commands. Dakota had dominated her, taken her to places she never dreamed possible, and now she wanted to return the gift. When reason returned, she reached for the vee between Dakota's legs, the mere brush of her fingers over the denim causing a low growl to emanate from Dakota's throat.

"Like that, do ya?"

"Yes," Dakota hissed.

"How about this?" Shawn squeezed.

"Fuck!"

"And this?" Shawn knelt between Dakota's legs, running her palms firmly along Dakota's thighs, traveling up to her center, where she pressed both her thumbs along the length of her. Dakota arched her back, whimpering when Shawn leaned forward to bite at the seam running directly over her clitoris.

"Oh, baby...you can't..."

"Oh, yes, I can. And I will."

Dakota groaned. "Shawn...you're making...me...Oh, man...come."

Shawn reacted to the urgency in Dakota's voice and quickly pulled off her jeans. She forced Dakota's thighs apart, tracing the swollen tissues with her tongue, ignoring her clitoris as it strained for attention.

"No more teasing." Dakota gripped the sheets. "Please, suck me. Do it."

Shawn finally took mercy on Dakota and drew her firmly into her mouth. It took only a few determined strokes for her to stiffen and cry Shawn's name.

"You're unbelievable," Dakota finally said, pulling Shawn up to lie next to her. "I have no control with you."

"Actually, I was thinking the same thing about you."

"Yeah?"

"Absolutely."

Dakota kissed her tenderly. "I need to tell you something."

"What is it?" She stroked Dakota's face. "Baby, what? You're crying."

"I love you."

"Oh, baby." Shawn pulled her close. "I love you too. With everything in me."

"I've never said it before. Never meant it so much. You're the one, Shawn."

"I always want to be the one. The only one."

"Don't ever doubt it." Dakota guided Shawn over her, sliding a hand between them, connecting them once again in body and soul. "I'm yours."

About the Author

L.T. Marie is a career athlete who writes during her free time. Her hobbies are reading every lesbian romance she can get her hands on, working out, and watching Giants baseball. *Three Days* is her first published work.

Books Available From Bold Strokes Books

Three Days by L.T. Marie. In a town like Vegas where anything can happen, Shawn and Dakota find that the stakes are love at all costs, and it's a gamble neither can afford to lose. (978-1-60282-569-7)

Swimming to Chicago by David-Matthew Barnes. As the lives of the adults around them unravel, high school students Alex and Robby form an unbreakable bond, vowing to do anything to stay together—even if it means leaving everything behind.(978-1-60282-572-7)

Hostage Moon by AJ Quinn. Hunter Roswell thought she had left her past behind, until a serial killer begins stalking her. Can FBI profiler Sara Wilder help her find her connection to the killer before he strikes on blood moon? (978-1-60282-568-0)

Erotica Exotica: Tales of Magic, Sex, and the Supernatural, edited by Richard Labonté. Today's top gay erotica authors offer sexual thrills and perverse arousal, spooky chills, and magical orgasms in these stories exploring arcane mystery, supernatural seduction, and sex that haunts in a manner both weird and wondrous. (978-1-60282-570-3)

Blue by Russ Gregory. Matt and Thatcher find themselves in the crosshairs of a psychotic killer stalking gay men in the streets of Austin, and only a 103-year-old nursing home resident holds the key to solving the murders—but can she give up her secrets in time to save them? (978-1-60282-571-0)

Balance of Forces: Toujours Ici by Ali Vali. Immortal Kendal Richoux's life began during the reign of Egypt's only female pharaoh, and history has taught her the dangers of getting too close to anyone who hasn't harnessed the power of time, but as she prepares for the most important battle of her long life, can she resist her attraction to Piper Marmande? (978-1-60282-567-3)

Contemporary Gay Romances by Felice Picano. This collection of short fiction from legendary novelist and memoirist Felice Picano are as different from any standard "romances" as you can get, but they will linger in the mind and memory. (978-1-60282-639-7)

Pirate's Fortune: Supreme Constellations Book Four by Gun Brooke. Set against the backdrop of war, captured mercenary Weiss Kyakh is persuaded to work undercover with bio-android Madisyn Pimm, which foils her plans to escape, but kindles unexpected love. (978-1-60282-563-5)

Sex and Skateboards by Ashley Bartlett. Sex and skateboards and surfing on the California coast. What more could anyone want? Alden McKenna thinks that's all she needs, until she meets Weston Duvall. (978-1-60282-562-8)

Waiting in the Wings by Melissa Brayden. Jenna has spent her whole life training for the stage, but the one thing she didn't prepare for was Adrienne. Is she ready to sacrifice what she's worked so hard for in exchange for a shot at something much deeper? (978-1-60282-561-1)

Wings: Subversive Gay Angel Erotica, edited by Todd Gregory. A collection of powerfully written tales of passion and desire centered on the aching beauty of angels. (978-1-60282-565-9)

Suite Nineteen by Mel Bossa. Psychic Ben Lebeau moves into Shilts Manor, where he meets seductive Lennox Van Kemp and his clan of Métis—guardians of a spiritual conspiracy dating back to Christ. But are Ben's psychic abilities strong enough to save him? (978-1-60282-564-2)

Speaking Out: LGBTQ Youth Stand Up, edited by Steve Berman. Inspiring stories written for and about LGBTQ teens of overcoming adversity (against intolerance and homophobia) and experiencing life after "coming out." (978-1-60282-566-6)

Forbidden Passions by MJ Williamz. Passion burns hotter when it's forbidden, and the fire between Katie Prentiss and Corrine Staples in antebellum Louisiana is raging out of control. (978-1-60282-641-0)

Harmony by Karis Walsh. When Brook Stanton meets a beautiful musician who threatens the security of her conventional, predetermined future, will she take a chance on finding the harmony only love creates? (978-1-60282-237-5)

Nightrise by Nell Stark and Trinity Tam. In the third book in the everafter series, when Valentine Darrow loses her soul, Alexa must cross continents to find a way to save her. (978-1-60282-238-2)

Men of the Mean Streets, edited by Greg Herren and J.M. Redmann. Dark tales of amorality and criminality by some of the top authors of gay mysteries. (978-1-60282-240-5)

Women of the Mean Streets, edited by J.M. Redmann and Greg Herren. Murder, mayhem, sex, and danger—these are the stories of the women who dare to tackle the mean streets. (978-1-60282-241-2)

Firestorm by Radclyffe. Firefighter paramedic Mallory "Ice" James isn't happy when the undisciplined Jac Russo joins her command, but lust isn't something either can control—and they soon discover ice burns as fiercely as flame. (978-1-60282-232-0)

The Best Defense by Carsen Taite. When socialite Aimee Howard hires former homicide detective Skye Keaton to find her missing niece, she vows not to mix business with pleasure, but she soon finds Skye hard to resist. (978-1-60282-233-7)

After the Fall by Robin Summers. When the plague destroys most of humanity, Taylor Stone thinks there's nothing left to live for, until she meets Kate, a woman who makes her realize love is still alive and makes her dream of a future she thought was no longer possible. (978-1-60282-234-4)

Accidents Never Happen by David-Matthew Barnes. From the moment Albert and Joey meet by chance beneath a train track on a street in Chicago, a domino effect is triggered, setting off a chain reaction of murder and tragedy. (978-1-60282-235-1)

In Plain View, edited by Shane Allison. Best-selling gay erotica authors create the stories of sex and desire modern readers crave. (978-1-60282-236-8)

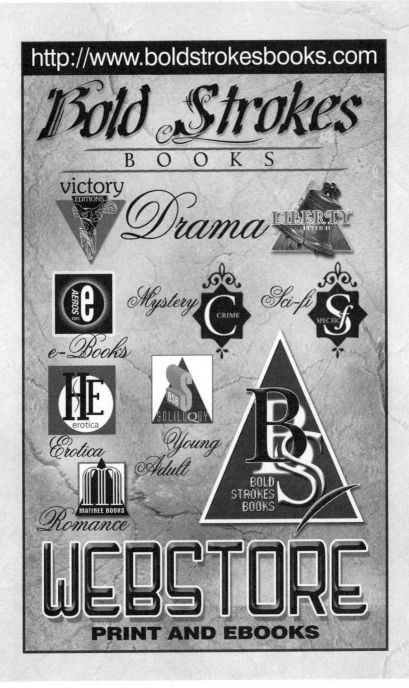